THE DISAPPEARANCE OF EDWIN DROOD

Also by Peter Rowland

The Last Liberal Governments
(Barrie & Jenkins, two volumes, 1968 and 1971)
Lloyd George (Barrie & Jenkins, 1975)

Compilations for the Folio Society:
Macaulay's History of England 1485–1685 (1985)
Macaulay's History of England 1702–1832 (1980)
My Early Times
(the autobiography of Charles Dickens (1988))

THE DISAPPEARANCE
OF EDWIN DROOD

Peter Rowland

St. Martin's Press
New York

Library of Congress Cataloging-in-Publication Data

Rowland, Peter.
    The disappearance of Edwin Drood / Peter Rowland.
      p.   cm.
    "A Thomas Dunne book."
    ISBN 0-312-06953-7
    I. Title.
  PR6068.0915D5   1992
  823'.914—dc20   91-40336
                                                 CIP

First published in Great Britain by Constable & Company Ltd.

To the memories of
Willoughby Matchett
(*The Dickensian*, January 1914, p.14)
and S.C. Roberts
(Introduction to OUP edition of
The Mystery of Edwin Drood, p. x)

AUTHOR'S NOTE

'I am lost without my Boswell,' Sherlock Holmes once remarked.

The private papers of Dr John H. Watson, MD, late of the Indian army, are less voluminous than those bequeathed to a delighted posterity by the Laird of Auchinleck, but the question of their publication has posed problems of a more intractable nature. Their trustees, Messrs Cox & Co. of Charing Cross, have been advised that, the passage of many years notwithstanding, there are certain matters over which, even now, the veil of secrecy must remain firmly drawn. Such material as it has otherwise been possible to release has proved, in the main, disappointingly inconsequential.

Frustrating though this is for the dedicated researcher, anxious to sift the contents of that battered tin despatch box to his heart's content, there occasionally occur relaxations of the necessary constraints. Specified time limits expire and the records of a particular case can pass, at last, into the public domain. One such case-history is set out in the pages that follow. The present editor was intrigued to find,

7

however, when perusing the manuscript, that parts of the story it had to tell, albeit incomplete and written from a totally different viewpoint, had already been chronicled elsewhere. Dr Watson's account, while a complete dossier in its own right, thus acquired something of a complementary character. This being so, I have taken the liberty of replacing its original title, 'The Adventure of the Missing Nephew', by one which (in the circumstances) appeared more appropriate. Other than this, editorial emendations have been kept to a minimum.

1

'Well, Watson, and what do you make of it?' enquired Holmes languidly, from the depths of his favourite armchair.

I pulled my own chair nearer the fire, digested the letter for a second time and passed it back with a shrug of the shoulders. 'Not a great deal,' I confessed. 'Your correspondent is obviously distraught and excited. Somebody – his son, presumably, or even a grandson – has left home and he is desperately anxious to find him. The notepaper is of good quality and the writer appears to be a man of substance, although the shakiness of the hand suggests someone of advancing years.'

The document in question, embossed with the address of 'The Gate House, Cloisterham' and dated 22 December 1894, was relatively brief. 'My Dear Sir,' it ran, 'I implore your assistance. You are the only person who can help me now. I must know, for my own peace of mind, whether my dear boy is alive or dead. This never-ending anxiety is driving me to the depths of insanity and despair. Only you, Mr Holmes, can solve this most baffling of problems.

9

Expense is no object. I will be with you tomorrow afternoon and beg that you will do me the honour of hearing my story and assisting me with every means at your disposal. I am, yours distractedly, John Jasper.'

'I fear', said Holmes, 'that since my much-publicized return to Baker Street those little articles by which you sought to bring my modest achievements in the sphere of elementary analysis and elucidation to the attention of a wider audience, although penned with the best of motives, are proving a mixed blessing. There appears to be an ominous disposition on the part of Mr Jasper to regard me, first and foremost, as a bureau for missing persons.'

'But he does refer', I remarked rather tartly, 'to an element of mystery in this affair, which is surely why he is coming to you, and he insists that you are the only person who can help him. I trust I am not to be blamed, Holmes, for attracting clients to your door at a time when you would otherwise be complaining of the dearth of business.'

Holmes smiled. 'The festive season', he said, 'does indeed have its *longueurs*. If Mr Jasper can relieve the ravages of boredom then he is most welcome, but my experience of reuniting fathers or grandfathers with long-lost heirs is limited and I rather fancy that I will be obliged, at the end of the day, to direct the gentleman elsewhere.' He glanced at his watch and then again at the letter, holding it up to the fading light. 'It may just be,' he mused, 'that this affair will not be totally devoid of points of interest. The note-paper, as you say, is of good quality, although sicklied o'er by a certain yellowish tinge which suggests a degree

10

of antiquity. You will observe that the date has been squeezed in as an afterthought and is penned in a different hand. A wife or secretary, perhaps? Cloisterham, as you are doubtless aware, is a cathedral city in Kent some forty miles hence. The dog-eared envelope which contained this letter, however, bears a Surrey postmark. Whether or not a curious address such as 'The Gate House' confirms that our client is a man of financial stature remains to be seen.'

We did not have to remain long in suspense, for the bell rang even as Holmes ruminated and a few minutes later Mrs Hudson ushered Mr John Jasper of Cloisterham into our room. He was a tall man, dressed in a long black coat which had evidently seen better days — and so, one was obliged to acknowledge, had Mr Jasper himself. His age was difficult to determine. His hair, once black, was heavily streaked with grey and there was an appalling haggardness about his features. The most striking aspect of the man was his dark eyes, which shone with an almost fanatical light. He collapsed with an air of exhaustion into the chair which I speedily made available and sat there without speaking for several minutes, breathing heavily. He eventually proffered a shaking hand and scrutinized each of us closely.

A look of mild surprise had passed across Holmes's face. 'I believe, sir,' he murmured, 'that you and I may have met some years ago, and in rather curious circumstances, but no matter — you will not recall the occasion. My name is Sherlock Holmes and this is my friend and colleague Dr Watson. You may speak freely in front of him and you have my assurance, if you so desire it, that what you say will not

11

go beyond the four walls of this room. How may we be of service?'

Mr Jasper summoned up his strength, drew a deep breath, and launched into his tale.

2

'You must understand, Mr Holmes,' began our visitor, fixing my colleague with a gaze which, until the end of his narrative, never wavered in its steadiness and intensity, 'that I am a well-known and, I hope I might say, respected resident of Cloisterham. I am a music-master and also the choir-master at the Cathedral – although in recent months I have been unable, I must confess, to execute my duties with that degree of efficiency which would normally have been my wont.

'Many years ago my only sister, Elizabeth, married a Mr Martin Drood, an enterprising young business man who was building up an engineering partnership with far-reaching commitments in Egypt – developing, it seems, some ingenious contrivances of major significance for the sanitation of that country, but I confess I am unfamiliar with the precise details. The Levant was, at that time, not only an extremely unhealthy but also a singularly dangerous part of the world – little more than five years, indeed, had elapsed since the crisis engendered by Mehemet Ali had threatened to plunge the whole region into turmoil. Elizabeth, her parents' forebodings and distress notwithstanding, insisted on accompanying Martin back to Egypt and it was in Alexandria, a year or so later, that she gave birth to a son. The climate was, however, already far too severe for one totally unsuited to such latitudes. Fatally weakened by the additional demands now made upon a feeble body, she gave up the ghost while Edwin was less than a month old. Martin, heartbroken by this event, found himself unable to continue his business activities with anything like his previous zeal. He returned to England, a shadow of his former self, and became little more than a sleeping partner in the firm which he had done so much to create. The wheels which he had helped to set in motion were turning, however, with alacrity and he was now a comparatively wealthy man. He eventually settled in Cloisterham (with some idea, I suppose, of consoling Elizabeth's parents for the loss of their daughter by presenting them with a grandson) and it is, indeed, in Cloisterham that he is buried, for he followed his wife to the grave within the space of twelve years.

'This is a melancholy tale, Mr Holmes, and I will endeavour to be brief. My parents, although well advanced in years, lavished upon Edwin all the love and attention that they had formerly bestowed upon Elizabeth and myself. They set in hand the necessary arrangements for his education, first at the very best of our public schools and then, later, at an engineering college in the north (for it was Martin's dying wish that his son should inherit his partnership and make good the family contribution to the regeneration of Egypt), with the result that Edwin came to Cloisterham only at comparatively rare intervals. Both my

14

parents died, however, before he could complete his studies and I myself then became his guardian. The intention was, indeed, that I should remain in that position until Edwin came of age, which would have been in the spring of this year. The engineering firm founded by his father continued to thrive and the annual income derived from that firm more than sufficed for his requirements. It was understood that, on the day that Edwin attained his majority, he would come into full and untrammelled possession of his inheritance. But that day, alas, is now seven months behind us, and whether or not that majority was actually attained is a question upon which, so far as I know, no one in this land is able to pronounce.

'But I anticipate. I must explain at this point that the dearest friend of Martin Drood, since their days at college together, was a Mr Ronald Bud who was also a widower and who also died young. He left behind him a seven-year-old daughter, four years Edwin's junior. The two young men, united in friendship and bereavement, made a compact before Ronald died to the effect that their entwined destinies should not terminate with the grave — for they recognized, already, that their own respective days were numbered — but should continue after death and bear fruit, as it were, in their children. It was agreed, in short, that the two potential orphans, Edwin and Rosa Bud, should (under the terms of their fathers' wills) be betrothed and that they should marry as soon as Edwin came of age. Such an arrangement might well seem strange in this day and age, but it was one born purely of a great friendship between two men whose emotions, agitated by great stress, were running at a fevered pitch – and it was accepted, indeed, that if the two young people, filial obligations notwithstanding, did not choose to unite in matrimony then there should be no compulsion upon them, financial or otherwise, to do so. The proposed arrangement was a sentimental one, expressive of their fathers' dearest hopes, but in no sense a legal commitment. Neither of them would be a penny the worse off if a union did not take place.

'So Mr Bud died and so Martin died and Rosa became the ward of a Mr Grewgious and I myself, in due course, became the guardian of Edwin. Miss Bud came to Cloisterham, where she was, until recently, a boarder at the Nuns' House, a seminary for young ladies run by a Miss Twinkleton. I myself kept a fatherly eye on her, in the capacity of music-master, and Mr Grewgious (a trustee of some description) came down from London from time to time to observe her progress. Edwin too came down to Cloisterham, when his obligations in town would permit, and invariably stayed with me at the Gate House – a bachelor apartment in close proximity to the Cathedral, where I have lived since my parents died. Relations between himself and Rosa appeared to be, so far as the outside world was concerned, all that their fathers could have wished and it was generally assumed that, when Edwin came of age, he and Rosa would marry and would then set sail for Egypt, where he would resume his father's commitments in the engineering profession.

'Ned – for so I almost invariably addressed the dear boy – had become, by this time, a living likeness of his father and had inherited, I must acknowledge, some of his father's slightly less attractive traits. In him they were, I fancy, little more than the impetuosities of youth and I am sure that he would soon have grown out of them, but a stranger meeting Ned for the first time would have found him – how shall we say? – somewhat bumptious, rather too self-assured for his years and perhaps inclined to speak casually or even carelessly of what others would have regarded as subjects more appropriate for graver discourse – subjects, certainly, that would have been accorded, in other quarters, a greater degree of respect or even reverence than Ned was apparently prepared to grant them.

'As ill luck would have it, there was indeed a stranger who encountered Ned for the first time in the autumn of last year – such a cursed stranger, I must confess, as I wish with all my heart had never left his native Ceylon – and that stranger was a young man called Neville Landless. From the moment that they first met there was bad blood between them. This dark young man appeared on the scene as the darkest of malign spirits and from the instant I clapped eyes on him I never knew a moment's peace of mind.

'Landless and his twin sister, Helena, were new arrivals in this country and had been sent to Cloisterham to complete their eduction – Helena at the Nuns' House and Neville under the guardianship of the Reverend Septimus Crisparkle, a Minor Canon who lives a short distance from myself. Ned and I were present at a dinner to welcome the young couple and after it had finished Ned and Landless escorted Miss Bud and Miss Landless back to the Nuns' House. The young ladies having left them, they instantly fell to quarrelling. Landless, it seems, took strong exception to some innocent enough expressions uttered by Ned and Ned responded angrily to what he regarded as his assailant's confounded impertinence. I chanced upon them at this stage and, in an effort to pour oil on troubled waters, insisted that they compose their difference and join me in a nightcap. A surly reconciliation (on Landless's part that is, not Ned's) was followed by a frightening scene within my very own sitting-room, when Landless physically attacked my dear boy, with the ferocity of a tiger, and had to be hauled away from him and evicted from the premises. Ned was shaken, although otherwise unhurt, but from that point onwards I went in fear of his life. It was a great relief to me, I do assure you, when Ned returned to London the following day.

'But Ned came back to Cloisterham two months later and I was prevailed upon, by Mr Crisparkle, to make one further attempt at composing relations between himself and Landless. On Christmas Eve, therefore, I played host to both of them at a convivial little dinner party and to all intents and purposes each of them was on his best behaviour and amicable relations were finally restored. But it was a night, Mr Holmes, of a terrible storm, which — although mercifully short-lived — wreaked havoc in the town while it lasted. (The Cathedral roof, to this day, bears some of the scars then inflicted on it.) At midnight my little party broke up, by which time the wind and rain had subsided to some extent. Ned announced that, before going to bed, he would stroll down to the river to observe the extent to which it had overflowed its banks. He invited Landless to accompany him and the latter agreed. The two of them left my gatehouse and that was the last occasion on which I ever saw my dear boy.

'Ned never returned home that night. I waited for many hours, endeavouring to convince myself that all was well and that, bearing in mind the impetuous nature of youth, he and Landless had perhaps returned to Minor Canon Corner (the home of Mr Crisparkle) to while away the early hours in conversation – perhaps, indeed, even to crack a further bottle or two, although intoxicating liquors at Minor Canon Corner are, I suspect, something of a rarity. When dawn finally broke, however, I felt that all was *not* well and that the time had finally come when I could no longer disguise from myself that something was dreadfully amiss. I eventually went to Minor Canon Corner, only to find that Landless had left there some hours before, while it was still dark, on what he was pleased to describe as a walking holiday. A party of volunteers immediately went in pursuit of him and he was apprehended at a spot some eight miles away. He resisted arrest, putting up a violent fight in the process, but was overpowered and brought back to myself and Mr Crisparkle. There was blood on his clothes, Mr Holmes, although he claimed that this was a result of the most recent fracas, and he denied that he had ever laid a finger on my dear Ned. They had, according to his account, surveyed the river and then strolled back to my gatehouse, Landless leaving him at the very entrance. To my own mind he was guilt personified, although the powers-that-be were less convinced and charges, I am sorry to say, have never been brought against him. He continues to protest his innocence.

'From that day to this, Mr Holmes, Ned has never been seen. Local volunteers scoured the area for him, and the river was dragged, but all to no avail. My boy had seemingly disappeared into thin air. He never returned to his London lodgings and his associates in town are as baffled as the residents of Cloisterham as to what could have become of him. Notices have been published, imploring him – if he was still in the land of the living – to make contact with me, but there has been no response – and I am certain, in my heart of hearts, that I will never see him again in this life. We were as close as two kinsmen could possibly be and I know that the thought always uppermost in my dear boy's mind was to spare me, if he possibly could, a moment's worry. Yet if he is dead, Mr Holmes, *where is the body?*'

3

There was a moment's silence after our client had finished.

'Curious indeed,' agreed Holmes. 'Are you able to explain to me, Mr Jasper, why it is that your nephew and Mr Landless should have fallen out in this unfortunate manner?'

Jasper stiffened. 'Is it really necessary for you to know that?' he asked.

'I think that the more I ascertain from the outset about this mysterious affair the greater chance there is of a solution emerging.'

'Very well then. The cause of the original altercation between them centred upon Miss Bud. Landless, although meeting her on only one occasion, appears to have formed an intense attachment to the young lady from the very first moment of that meeting – I suspect that the number of his female acquaintances is limited – and bitterly resented the fact that she was on the point of becoming engaged to Ned. Inflamed by passion and jealousy, he suggested that Ned was treating her in rather too casual a fashion and making light of something that ought to be held in much greater esteem.'

'And how has the young lady herself reacted to her fiancée's disappearance?'

Our client was silent for a moment and then spoke with the air of one choosing his words with great deliberation. 'She was, of course, greatly distressed and agitated. But I am unable to speak from first-hand knowledge about her present state of mind. She left Cloisterham several months ago and now resides somewhere in London.'

'You are aware of her precise location?'

'Unfortunately, no. On one point, however, I feel obliged to correct you. Miss Bud and my nephew, although seemingly predestined for one another from their earliest days, never reached the point of becoming formally betrothed. On the day before he disappeared Ned and she agreed, by mutual consent, that they were not really suited and that they should part as friends, to live henceforth in a relationship of brother and sister.'

'I see. Would Mr Landless have been aware of this?'

'I doubt it.'

'Were *you* aware of it?'

Again, a moment's silence before the answer came – and, when it did, it was as though it had been wrung out of Mr Jasper's innermost depths. 'No.' (Uttered hoarsely, with great emotion.)

Holmes deliberated for a while. 'Has any consideration been given', he asked, 'to the possibility that Mr Drood may have lost his memory?'

'It is, I suppose, possible,' said Mr Jasper, with the air of one who did not for one moment consider that this was remotely likely. He paused for a moment, engaged in some

22

internal wrestle with himself, and then added, 'To tell the truth, Mr Holmes, I did at one time almost succeed in convincing myself that Ned had chosen to disappear of his own accord.'

'And why would he have done that?'

'Because the dear boy (so I ascertained afterwards) had feared for my peace of mind on learning that his unofficial engagement to Miss Bud would never be ratified. He had intended, in fact, that the news should be broken to me by Mr Grewgious – as, indeed, it was, but in circumstances very different from those which Ned had envisaged.'

'But you no longer believe that?'

Mr Jasper shook his head vigorously. 'Not since that moment . . .' he began, paused for an instant and then resumed in stronger voice. 'Not since that moment when Edwin's gold watch, with the chain still attached to it, together with his shirt-pin, were found in the river.'

Holmes sat bolt upright. 'Indeed! This is something that you have omitted to mention. Pray, where was this, Mr Jasper?'

'At Cloisterham Weir, some two miles upstream from that part of the river which Ned and Landless had intended to visit that night.'

'And who found them?'

'Mr Crisparkle, a week or two after Edwin's disappearance. There was no doubt as to their ownership – the watch bore the initials E. D. and was instantly identified as belonging to Ned. That he should have thrown them away himself is inconceivable.'

'Unless, indeed, he had determined to start a new life in

every respect, although without an intimate knowledge of the young gentleman's state of mind on the night it is difficult to judge why this might be.' Holmes pondered for a time. 'And is there anything else you wish to bring to my attention?'

'There is, and yet I scarcely know how to put it into words. Strange things have been happening in Cloisterham in recent weeks, Mr Holmes. I feel, somehow, as though a conspiracy were being waged against me, although it is difficult to pinpoint how it has developed or who the instigators are. I feel, almost, as though I were being put on trial. Attitudes have stiffened. People whom I have long been accustomed to look upon as friends treat me in a cold, antagonistic fashion – almost as though they suspected that *I* might have something to do with my dear boy's disappearance! Fingers are being pointed and remarks are being whispered. The most tangible development of all, perhaps, is that a stranger has appeared in the town – a genial old gentleman with a shock of white hair – who seems, all outward appearances to the contrary, to be keeping me under surveillance. He has moved into the house next door to mine and I see him wherever I go, try as I might to avoid him. You may feel, perhaps, that I am becoming deranged, and it may be that my nerves are now so finely stretched that it is difficult to distinguish between reality and imagination, but I do not feel' – and his voice broke at this point – 'that my equanimity can continue for very much longer. The uncertainty about Ned's fate needs to be resolved one way or the other. I am prepared for the worst, but it is the absence of knowledge about what

24

happened on that terrible night that is gradually consuming me. How much longer can I go on like this? I appeal to you to abandon whatever other investigations you may have in hand and come to my rescue!'

'And the name of this amiable but watchful old gentleman?'

'Datchery, Mr Holmes. Dick Datchery. He is a total stranger — retired from the diplomatic service, so he claims — who has announced his intention of ending his days in Cloisterham.'

Holmes ruminated for a moment and our client grew still more agitated. 'The point that I must impress upon you above all things', he urged, 'is that Neville Landless (also now residing in London, in the vicinity of Staples Inn) is undoubtedly the perpetrator of this foul deed. Proof, sir, is needed, proof above all things, so that we might bring the villain to justice!'

'We must lose no time,' said Holmes, 'even at this late hour, in familiarizing ourselves with the scene of these events.' He turned to me questioningly. 'Do you have any objection, Watson, to our spending Christmas away from London? The arrangement would not, I fancy, be altogether unwelcome to Mrs Hudson, who has dropped a pointed hint or two about her desire to share the yule-tide festivities with a married sister in Croydon, and a brief change of scene might well be what you yourself, in your professional capacity, would prescribe for two middle-aged gentlemen who are otherwise only too susceptible to the attractions of a fusty atmosphere and a blazing fire.'

I willingly indicated my assent.

'Then that's settled. It is a thousand pities, though, that the trail, if one still exists, was laid so long ago, for it is a year, almost to the very day, since Mr Drood disappeared. Had the matter been brought to my attention at an earlier stage I would have been better equipped to deal with it.'

Mr Jasper looked surprised. 'You must remember, Mr Holmes,' he pointed out, 'that until very recently the nation at large was under the firm impression that your remains were somewhere in the vicinity of the Reichenbach Falls. Until you were brought back to life, as it were, the possibility of my being able to consult you simply did not arise.'

'Recalled to life,' said Holmes sorrowfully, shaking his head. 'You are, of course, quite right and I apologize for my oversight. The whirligig of time plays strange tricks with the mind. Or it may be, of course, that the whirligig of the mind plays strange tricks with time.'

Our visitor, tiring of what he evidently regarded as tedious sophistries, rose to his feet. 'If you are only able to recall Ned to life,' he exclaimed, 'or to ascertain, once and for all, what became of the dear boy, I shall be everlastingly in your debt.'

'We shall be with you by tomorrow afternoon,' said Holmes. 'There is, I believe, a relatively frequent train service to Cloisterham, even on Christmas Eve, is there not?'

'Trains?' repeated Jasper blankly, his eyes taking on a curiously glazed expression. 'I know nothing of such matters. You must make your own arrangements.'

'But perhaps there is a suitable hostelry you can recommend?'

'The Crozier,' said our visitor with a slight touch of impatience. 'Mr Bastewell maintains a good house, I believe. But these are mundane matters, Mr Holmes, which can surely be left to Dr Watson's consideration. I implore you to concentrate your own unique faculties on what has happened to Ned and to ascertain, for better or worse, what has become of him.'

'Indeed I will,' said Holmes smoothly, seeing our client to the door. 'You may rest assured, Mr Jasper, that this most intriguing affair will receive our full attention. All being well, we three will meet again within a very few hours. In the mean time, I wish you good-night.' He closed the door and lapsed into silence.

'A perplexing affair,' I remarked, crossing to the window and gazing down at the Christmas shoppers who were now intermingling with the homeward-bound office workers of Baker Street. Night had fallen, the lamps had been lit, the shop fronts were illuminated and odd flakes of snow swirled and twirled upon the garish scene. Our client, having emerged from the door of 221B, stood still for a moment as though getting his bearings and then strode off in a northerly direction.

'Perplexing indeed,' came the thoughtful rejoinder, 'although it may be that our attentions have been attracted by different aspects of the story. Mr Jasper's memory is oddly selective. My history is a trifle rusty, and my knowledge of the pressures brought to bear upon respectable choir-masters is scanty in the extreme, but I cannot help wondering —'

'Holmes,' said I, 'there is something strange here. It seems that our client is being accosted.'

Holmes joined me at the window. Two men in bulky coats and bowler hats, emerging from the shadows of a doorway, had overtaken and stopped John Jasper and engaged him in conversation. There was what appeared to be a short altercation. Jasper rounded angrily upon them for a moment, his head jerked back in fury, and then he appeared to resign himself to their company and all three walked on together – Jasper in the centre – to be caught up in the throng.

Holmes, without a word, seized his coat, hurried from the room and hastened down the road in pursuit, elbowing his way through the crowds. The three figures were, by this time, hopelessly out of sight and he returned some twenty minutes later, shaking his head with a rueful expression. 'Not a trace of them,' he remarked. 'Truly, a curious end to a curious visit. We must see what the morrow brings forth.'

No more did he say that night but retired to his room. And, a little while later, I heard the melancholy sounds of a violin.

4

Holmes was already out and about when I awoke the following morning but he returned soon after eleven. 'Great George Street,' was his curt response to my inevitable question — and, on interrogative eyebrows being raised, patiently explained, 'The headquarters of the Institution of Civil Engineers. I also endeavoured', he added cryptically, 'to renew a relationship with a certain royal personage of my acquaintance, but it transpired that Her Majesty was out of town.' This was the limit of what could be extracted from him. He remained in an uncommunicative mood for the next few hours and I knew better, by this time, than to interrupt such silences. My curiosity about his views on the subject of Neville Landless, let alone the purposes of the two men who had joined John Jasper the previous evening, would have to remain unsatisfied.

Our valises packed, we took a cab to Charing Cross station. Cloisterham having been, quite literally, off the beaten track for the best part of thirty years, as a consequence of never having been on it, and surviving its exclusion with equanimity, it was only as an afterthought that it had occurred to the managers of the London and South East Region Railway Company that this small, sleepy town might be usefully encompassed within a network which had extended its tentacles to almost every other community between the capital and the south coast. Having thus encompassed it, they appeared to have almost instantly repented of their decision. The great majority of trains shot through the town without stopping at all and those that did deign to draw reluctantly to a halt also insisted, for reasons of a savage perversity that defied all rational explanation, on stopping for several minutes at every other station *en route* regardless of whether anyone alighted or anyone boarded. The journey to our destination thus proved abominably slow and it was not until the early evening that we finally found ourselves strolling through the chilly main thoroughfare of the old Cathedral city. Dusk was falling, lights twinkled through the curtains now being pulled in the small and ancient houses and a great silence, in marked contrast to the turmoil of London, surrounded us wherever we went. The number of individuals out and about were so few that our footsteps positively echoed from one side of the street to the other.

'There is the Cathedral,' I remarked, as a great grey shape with a dominating tower, feebly illumined from within, loomed up.

'And there', added Holmes, 'is Mr Jasper's gatehouse. Shrouded in darkness, I observe. Obviously our client is not at home, but on this day, of all the days of the year, I would not have expected him to be. There is presumably a service either in progress or due to start in the near future.'

The medieval gatehouse, at the end of the High Street, surmounted a road which veered sharply to the left and ran towards the inky blackness surrounding the Cathedral and its environs. Still, grim and silent, somewhat in the posture of a squat, bow-legged sentinel, the gatehouse maintained motionless watch on a scene which grew increasingly indistinct. I shivered, involuntarily, and then brightened as I glimpsed our first port of call (its location ascertained from enquiries at the station) coming into view. 'The Crozier!' I exclaimed. 'And, all being well, a splendid repast with which to round off the day.'

The crowded interior of The Crozier was, indeed, all that one could have wished for in the way of a comfortable, old-fashioned, Kentish inn, and mine host, a plump, rubicund man, greeted us with a welcoming smile. 'Two pints of your best ale if you please, landlord,' said Holmes, loosening his overcoat and warming his hands by the fire. 'Have I the pleasure of addressing Mr Bastewell?'

Mine host, presenting us with two foaming tankards, looked puzzled. 'No, sir,' he said. 'There's no one of that name here, and *I've* been here the best part of fifteen years. Name of Appleby, sir. Never heard of no Bastewell.'

'No matter,' said Holmes. 'A small misunderstanding, obviously. More to the point, Mr Appleby, are you able to furnish us with a room for the next night or two? If your accommodation is as good as your ale, I fancy we'll have no complaints!'

The landlord's face dropped. 'Eeeh, sirs! I'm that sorry,' he exclaimed. 'Normally there'd have been no difficulty, but at this time of all times . . . If you'd only let us know you were

31

coming, a week or two back, I'm sure we could have fitted you in somewhere, but nowabouts it's a bit too late in the day, I'm thinking. It's the Convention, you see. You haven't come for the Convention yourselves, have you?' he asked with a sudden burst of hopefulness.

Holmes looked blank. 'What Convention's this?' I asked.

'Why of the Admirers, don't you see!'

Both of us now looked blank and Mr Appleby hastened to explain. A very great author, it seemed, had once lived in close proximity to Cloisterham and had died at this country home almost twenty-five years before — to be precise, twenty-four years and six months before. The Admirers of the great author had come together to pay homage, as it were, on the eve of this sad anniversary year, the Christmas period providing a suitable opportunity for the Admirers to converge from far and near.

'And what do they actually *do*?' I asked.

'Do, sir? Why, read chapters of his books out loud to one another and enjoy them and discuss them, like.'

'And that is the full extent of their activity?' asked Holmes, in some perplexity.

'Why bless me, no sir! That's the serious part of their proceedings, the sedentary aspect of their carryings-on if you take my meaning, sir.' And, on our still looking puzzled, the landlord explained that the Admirers also spent a considerable part of their time in dressing up as characters from the great novelist's books, in re-enacting scenes from those books, in processing through the streets in their period costumes and in feasting and revelry. And, to lend pictorial force to his explanations, there was at this point a sudden irruption of a group of the Admirers into that section of the inn. They were indeed in frolicsome mood, attired in costumes of a bygone age and bubbling over with seasonable goodwill. A seemingly elderly gentleman, a nightshirt pulled over his ordinary clothes and with an improbable shock of white hair, exclaimed, 'Bah, humbug!' two or three times, at which the other Admirers convulsed themselves with mirth, and they disappeared into a separate part of the inn which had been, so we gathered, especially set aside for their festivities.

'A singular but, I suppose, harmless pursuit,' said Holmes, shaking his head, as we took our seats in the dining-room — for the landlord had hastened to assure us that, while beds were in sadly short supply, he could offer us food in abundance. The meal that followed was all that we could have wished for and we devoured it in satisfaction. Holmes pushed back his plate, poured himself a fresh glass of brandy and groped for his brier pipe in absent-minded fashion. 'A curious state of affairs,' he murmured, almost to himself, as he filled it.

'You mean the disappearance of Mr Drood?'

'No, my dear chap; a strange business, certainly, but I refer to the activities of our friends in the adjoining apartments. That they should go to such lengths! Fact is fact and fiction is fiction and the dividing line between their respective territories should never be traversed. To mix one with the other is to meddle with the natural order of things,' He puffed contentedly and warmed to his theme, unconsciously making amends, perhaps, for his silence earlier in the day. 'Characters such as Don Quixote and Sancho Panza, say, loom larger than life in our imaginations, but if you and I were to encounter them walking towards us down Cloisterham High Street I fear we would almost certainly be sadly disillusioned. They would be mere mortals, the same as ourselves — for to make them, literally, larger than life (as our American cousins might be disposed to do, in their natural enthusiasm for such enterprises) would be to make them grotesques. Characters from Fact, similarly, should not be allowed to stray into the realm of Fiction, although historical romances — with the author of *Waverley* as an outstanding offender — have tended to obliterate the frontier to so great an extent that it is difficult to determine where the boundary now lies.'

'Perhaps', I suggested, 'we should draw a distinction between, say, the monarchs of Fact and the monarchs of Fiction? Between the Queen Elizabeth portrayed in our history books and the Queen Elizabeth portrayed in our novels?'

'That, certainly, is one solution, but scarcely a satisfactory one. The great majority of readers will surely be unable to distinguish between the genuine article and the counterfeit, with the fictional version aping the original model in every conceivable degree yet being, in the last analysis, nothing more than a two-dimensional pasteboard figure, incapable of doing anything that might be considered even remotely out of character. You and I, Watson, thanks to those little case-histories of yours which have attracted so much attention in recent times, are in some danger of being immortalized! Who will be able to tell, a hundred years from now, whether we were Fact or Fiction? Dare we contemplate what enormities, what fabulous exploits, might not be perpetrated in our names? Will there even be', he added with a shudder, 'duplicate versions of myself perambulating the environs of Baker Street at dead of night, equipped with deerstalker hats, bloodhounds and magnifying glasses and accompanied by their faithful Watsons?'

'Holmes,' said I, laughing, 'you are becoming altogether too fanciful in your old age (or in your cups), although – in general terms – I take your point. And as with persons,' I added, 'so, I suppose, with places.'

'Exactly. The London, say, of Fiction may closely resemble the London of Fact and may run on seemingly parallel lines, but it is a distinct entity and the two should never be confused. The Reverend Charles Dodgson came close to defining the situation with his creation of Looking-Glass Land, where – at first glance – the state of affairs on the other side of the mirror is basically the same as that of the real world, but should an Alice venture to intrude into that other world she will soon discover that things are strangely different. The same principle also applies, of course, to the weather. In this country a white Christmas is the rarest of events, for which we may be profoundly thankful, but when did you last peruse a Christmas tale set in England in which the snow was not falling fast or, at any rate, lying thick upon the ground? – and similar liberties may be taken, by our novelists, with the days of the week or even with the months of the year. But I have held forth for far too long and it is high time we were making a move. With no room at the inn on Christmas Eve, of all nights, we must exercise our ingenuity to its uttermost if we are to secure a roof for our heads.'

Mine host, with reiterated apologies, bowed us out (a lugubrious gentleman in the background, attired in the rustic garb of a bygone age, meanwhile making so bold as to inform us that he was willin' and being instantly hauled out of sight by unseen hands, amidst peals of recriminatory laughter from fellow Admirers) and we found ourselves walking, once again, through the deserted streets of Cloisterham as the Cathedral clock chimed the ninth hour of the night.

5

The night had become appreciably colder, and pulling our coats about us we retraced our steps to the gatehouse. It was still in darkness. We climbed the postern stairs, which carried with them an odour of peculiar staleness. 'There is a gritty state of things here,' said Holmes, shuffling his feet. 'These steps have not been swept for some considerable time.' He struck a match and rapped on the uninviting door revealed by its feeble light, but answer came there none from Mr Jasper.

'Perhaps he is still at the Cathedral,' I suggested, after Holmes had knocked again and we had waited several minutes. My companion grunted. 'If so,' he remarked, 'it is an unconscionably long service.' We waited a little while longer, after a third and final knock, and then groped our way back to the fresher air of the outside world.

A brief survey now led to the discovery that, squeezed between the lower portion of the far side of the gatehouse and the High Street proper, barely wide enough for the slimmest of travellers to pass through, was an exceedingly narrow alleyway. Holmes ventured down it, I following close at his heels, and we found that a tiny door was set into the wall of the gatehouse. The chances of anyone being in residence in this part of the building seemed equally unpromising, but after Holmes had thundered on the door several times it opened a few inches and the face of a very old gentleman could be dimly discerned peeping out at us. I was half prepared for a testy cry of 'Here's a knocking indeed! Who's there, i' th' name of Beelzebub?' but the old man held his peace.

'Good evening,' roared Holmes. The face was unresponsive. 'I'm exceedingly sorry to trouble you at this late hour but you may be able to help us.'

The old gentleman continued to peer out suspiciously.

'We are friends of Mr Jasper, your next-door neighbour.'

''E ain't 'ere!' came the suddenly spirited reply, and the door began to close at a great rate.

Holmes, however, had adroitly inserted his foot in the limited space available before the operation could be completed. 'I realize that,' he shouted, 'but my friend and I have come a very long way and there is no room at the inn. We are desperately anxious for accommodation. Are you able to take us under your roof for just one night? We will pay you well.'

At this final announcement the door wavered and then began to swing cautiously open again. Holmes, pressing home his advantage, produced a couple of sovereigns and they found a ready market.

'Wait 'ere,' came the command and the old gentleman disappeared for several minutes, returning with a candle. He led us into what were two remarkably tiny rooms – bearing, indeed, a closer resemblance to miniature dungeons than to ordinary living quarters. We were evidently in chambers which had been created some four or five hundred years before. They were sparsely furnished in the extreme, but there was a bed, a chair, a table and a corner-cupboard, the last of these features being virtually built into the wall. There was also another door to the outside world. "Tain't much,' grumbled the old man, with the merest hint of an apology.

'On the contrary, this will suit us splendidly,' bellowed Holmes. I vigorously nodded my agreement. The old gentleman, having lit a small lamp, saw no need to exert himself further and began to withdraw. 'One moment, sir,' exclaimed Holmes. 'Are you able to enlighten my friend and myself as to the times of the Cathedral services? Would we be correct in assuming that there will be one at midnight and one at the crack of dawn tomorrow?'

The old gentleman drew himself up proudly. 'Man an' boy,' he declared, 'I've been working at this Cathedral for seventy years, and there ain't much that I don't know about times of services!'

We signified, unfeignedly, our astonishment at this announcement and the old gentleman, encouraged by our interest, became still more expansive. 'I've been', he proclaimed, 'chorister, lay clerk, under-verger and now verger. I knows that Cathedral like the back of me 'and. The Bishop himself has been known to consult me on occasion. "Mr Tope," says he, 'would I be right in assuming that . . ." or "Mr Tope," he says, "please correct me if I'm wrong, but . . .". "Your Grace," I've said to him many a time, "you've come to the right man, Your Grace", and so 'e 'as, and I've put him right on one or two points before now and will probably do so again – *and* the next man arter 'im! Bishops come and bishops go, but Tope goes on for ever.'

Our wonder and admiration knew, by this time, no bounds and Holmes marked the occasion by the production of another sovereign, which speedily joined its predecessors. Thus encouraged, Mr Tope confirmed that there was indeed a midnight and an early morning service and, his duties done, abruptly disappeared. Holmes flung himself upon the bed, lost in thought, and I opened up the cupboard doors in order to stow away our modest travelling accoutrements. I was intrigued to see that, on the inside of one of the doors, a number of vertical lines, of varying lengths, had been chalked and that, on the other, there appeared (also in chalk) the word KIN-FREE-DER-EL, the second syllable being underlined, followed by first a question mark and then an exclamation mark. I called Holmes's attention to these mysterious jottings and he evinced a mild interest in them. 'The lines', he said, 'would seem to be an example of an old country method of keeping a tally, or score, while "Kin-free-der-el" is perhaps a jocular rendition of the word "cathedral", although the humour of the translation escapes me for the moment. Is it the kin or the letter L from which one is being set free? Of more immediate interest, I would suggest, is the fact that we have a door of our own to the outside world through which we can come and go, during the next few hours, without the necessity of having to disturb our worthy host on each occasion. Now, Watson, are you game for a tour of inspection?'

I willingly consented. With the lamp extinguished, and the door on the latch, we emerged into the precincts of the Cathedral, at a point exactly opposite the entrance to John Jasper's staircase, and walked towards the massive building. The moon was, by this time, high in the sky, casting a white light over the churchyard with its tombs, graves, miniature mausoleums, broken columns, sorrowing angels and lachrymose cherubs, their eyes rolled upwards, frozen in lamentation. We made our way through this shimmering city of the dead. Although the tombstones were railed off from the footpath, which made it difficult to decipher any of the words on them, even had we been so inclined, it was impossible to ignore the fact that some of them were in a sorry state of disrepair.

'I have devised', said Holmes softly, 'a little catechism for you, Watson. Let us suppose you had been so unscrupulous as to purloin a valuable book (as distinct from a letter) and that you wished, in the limited amount of time available before a search began, to hide it where it would be most likely to escape attention. Where would you go?'

I considered for a moment. 'To a library?' I suggested.

'Excellent! Now, in the words of a distant clerical acquaintance, where would you hide a leaf?'

'In a forest of leaves.'

'Excellent again! And finally, Watson, where would you hide a body?'

'In a forest of bodies,' I murmured, drawing in my breath and gazing at the wrecked tombs beyond the railings.

Holmes nodded. 'I commend the thought to your consideration,' he remarked quietly.

We strolled on, circumnavigating the Cathedral and its environs, and found ourselves at Minor Canon Corner, where Neville Landless had lodged with Mr Crisparkle before his banishment to London. We then turned into what was the definitely non-ecclesiastical and far from salubrious atmosphere of Gas Works Gardens. From the door of a seedy lodging establishment half-way along (the Travellers' Tuppenny, so a ramshackle sign proclaimed) streamed out a ray of light and the sound of ribald singing and raucous laughter from the inmates – the first human voices, other than our own, that we had heard for the best part of an hour.

'There is, it seems, an unruly element in Cloisterham,' said Holmes with a smile.

'On reflection,' I ventured tentatively, after a few minutes' silence, 'I cannot help wondering whether we are perhaps not making rather heavy weather of this business. Mr Jasper's account held us enthralled, and he virtually convinced us that Landless was the man responsible for his nephew's disappearance, but might it not be that Drood was simply attacked and mortally injured by some ruffian from that establishment which we have just passed? A shocking event, admittedly, but a relatively mundane affair scarcely necessitating your own involvement.'

'I would judge it exceedingly unlikely. The most significant aspect of this curious tale, although Mr Jasper almost forgot to mention it, is the fact that Drood's watch and chain and shirt-pin were thrown in the river. That would seem to rule out robbery as a motive.'

'Unless', I pursued, 'the assailant panicked when he found that he had killed the young man and threw away these incriminating items lest they be found on him.'

'But in that case, where is the body? There are really only two possibilities. The first is that Drood divested himself of those items as a prelude to deliberately disappearing. That seems improbable, but cannot be ruled out completely. The second is that somebody else removed them so that a body, if discovered, would not be easily identified. That in itself, however, suggests one of two further possibilities: either that the body would not be found for a very long time indeed, in which case identification would be impossible, or that if it *were* to be found in a relatively short space of time it would somehow have been rendered unrecognizable by the process of decomposition being artificially accelerated. It may be that Mr Drood is, by this time, no more than the dust beneath our feet.'

We turned into the High Street for the second time that day, walking past the Nuns' House seminary which had been attended by Miss Bud, and − our immediate tour of inspection complete − fetched up at the gatehouse. There were now several groups of people converging on the Cathedral but Mr Jasper's quarters remained, as ever, in darkness.

'What now?' I asked.

'For you, Watson, the midnight service, for the witching hour is only twenty minutes away. It will doubtless be conducive to your spiritual well-being, but observe care-fully and see if you can perceive our friend among the members of the choir. (But his absence from last year's service leads me to suspect that he will also be absent on this occasion.) Note, too, the time at which the proceedings conclude.'

'And you, Holmes?'

'I shall remain here until midnight and then stroll down to gaze at the river – at about the same time, so we are given to understand, as Messrs Drood and Landless strolled down to gaze at it exactly twelve months ago.'

'You are aware of its location?'

Holmes smiled faintly. 'There is an ancient map of the locality on display in the entrance hall of The Crozier: the jubilant distractions of the Admirers notwithstanding, I took the opportunity of familiarizing myself with the geography of Cloisterham before we took our leave.'

I left him standing in the shadow of the gatehouse and returned to the Cathedral, finding myself in the company of a fair-sized congregation. The service was indeed impressive. The choir was in splendid form and 'Once in Royal David's City' pealed out on the organ at the stroke of midnight. But of Mr Jasper there was no sign.

I made my way back to the gatehouse at the conclusion of the service and Holmes joined me about twenty minutes later. There being, he reported, a total absence of the foul weather which had so disfigured the previous Christmas Eve, the river was in an unspectacular condition. He had seen no one on his return journey, the Cathedral worshippers and clergy having dispersed to their homes, which suggested that no one would have been abroad to see Drood and Landless the previous year. He had knocked for one last time at Mr Jasper's door but, once again, there had been no reply. 'It seems', he concluded, 'that we must search for a missing uncle as well as a missing nephew. Truly, a perplexing state of affairs! But the twenty-fifth day of December is upon us and a few hours' sleep will not come amiss. You take the bed, my dear fellow. The chair will suffice for my requirements.'

And a few minutes later, as soon as we had settled ourselves and I had extinguished the lamp, there rang through the darkness a cheery cry of 'Merry Christmas, Watson!'

6

I was awoken, rather to my surprise, by an elderly lady shaking me gently by the shoulder. I sat up in some confusion, to find that there was no sign of Holmes and that the old lady had set down a cup of tea on the small table beside the bed. I accepted it with hearty thanks, coupled with the compliments of the season, and Mrs Tope (for she then begged leave to introduce herself) watched me drink it with much satisfaction.

Had I slept well? she wanted to know. On my assuring her that I had she lingered a while, with the air of one who did not often have the opportunity for speaking to fresh acquaintances, and became quite confidential. We had been, she explained, the first people to stay at the Tope residence for many years, although the rooms were always kept ready for unexpected guests and there had been a time, indeed, when she had hoped that they might make a regular "go" of the lodging-house business. For some inexplicable reason, however, the two tiny chambers had not aroused any great enthusiasm among potential clientele and had failed to prove the little goldmine confidently expected. One of the last of their lodgers, however, and one who had stayed there for several weeks, off and on, had been a dear old gentleman who (like myself) was very fond of his tea. 'Tea is capital, Mrs Tope,' he had proclaimed on several occasions; 'I am exceedingly partial to it, and *your* tea is the finest in all Cloisterham.'

I hastened to assure her that, on the basis of my own experience, the old gentleman could surely not have been mistaken in his opinion. It was, indeed, one which I most certainly endorsed. Thus encouraged, Mrs Tope excused herself for a few minutes and returned with a *second* cup for my benefit. I downed it with as great an enthusiasm as I could muster and Mrs Tope, while keeping an observant eye upon me, continued to ruminate on the character of her last lodger. He was, it seemed, a retired gentleman, very genial and easy-going in' his ways although surprisingly active for a man of his years. But he must have been, all outward appearances to the contrary, an invalid. He had remarked several times towards the end, with a curious little smile, that he was living on borrowed time.

'Towards the end?' I queried.

'Towards the end of his stay here, sir.'

'Did he end his days in Cloisterham?' I enquired, more for some-thing to say than for reasons of any real curiosity on the subject.

'That was certainly his intention, sir, but it was all rather curious and, in a sense, I'm not able to say one way or the other. He came and went, not being a totally committed resident as it were, and there came a time when he went away and simply didn't come back, although paid up to the end of the following week. We didn't hear no more about him or from him, did Tope and me, and there was nothing of any consequence in these rooms to indicate whether he had relatives or forwarding addresses, but that was very many years ago now, sir, and I'm sure the old gentleman has passed on to wherever he was going by this time. It must have been in the autumn that he went,' she added rather inconsequentially, 'as he made some little joke about being in the autumn of our days when the leaves began to fall in the Close and that was one of the last times that I saw him.'

I could not help reflecting that the residents of Cloisterham were rather prone to disappear in unexpected fashion but I was tiring of the subject of Mrs Tope's last lodger and endeavoured to indicate, by a certain straightening of the back, that this was all very delightful but that it was high time that I was up and doing. The good lady instantly took the hint and, with a slight bob and an assurance that shaving water would be available whenever I required it, returned to her quarters.

Holmes reappeared a little while later, after I had finished dressing, and flung himself into the chair. The expression on his face was partly bemused and partly elated. He had, he announced, attended the early morning service. Again, the choir had been magnificent but there had been no sign of Mr Jasper. To my surprise, however, he dismissed this as a matter of no great significance. 'I have discovered', he announced, with undisguised relish, 'something that goes a long way towards explaining much that had been previously unclear – and, indeed, that confirms a suspicion that has been growing upon me from the moment that we arrived here.'

What this mysterious something was, however, he declined to reveal for the moment, but insisted that I immediately accompany him back to the Cathedral. Ablutions completed, we hastened out into the morning sunshine and returned to the churchyard, which looked far less eerie than on the previous evening. Holmes suddenly stopped, *en route* as it were to our final destination, and pointed at one particular monument. 'What do you think of that, Watson?' he asked with a smile.

The monument bore an inscription couched in terms of astonishing pomposity which proclaimed that it was dedicated to the memory of Ethelinda, departed this life in the month of December 1868, the Reverential Wife of Mr Thomas Sapsea, Auctioneer, Valuer, Estate Agent, &c., of the City of Cloisterham

Whose Knowledge of the World,
Though somewhat extensive,
Never brought him acquainted with
A SPIRIT
More capable of
LOOKING UP TO HIM.

The passing stranger was asked whether he could do likewise and sternly commanded, if the response were a negative one, to retire with a blush.

'I think', murmured Holmes abruptly, 'that we should act upon that final adjuration without delay.'

But it was too late. I suddenly became aware that, leaning

on a substantial stick a few yards away, a very elderly, somewhat portly gentleman had been observing our interest with evident satisfaction. He was dressed completely in black and equipped with so splendid a top hat and so imposingly gaitered that I felt, for a moment, that we could not possibly be in the presence of anyone less exalted than the Bishop himself.

'The greetings of the festive season,' roared this magnificent apparition. 'Chancing to pass this way on my way to morning worship, I could not help but observe that you felt compelled to linger at a memorial to a very simple but dear creature (gone these twenty-six years, gentlemen!) and to digest the sentiments so unworthily expressed thereon.'

'Indeed yes,' agreed Holmes with some enthusiasm. 'We were lost in admiration. But surely, my good sir, have I not the honour of addressing in person the author of those splendid sentiments? Is it really Mr Thomas Sapsea that I see before me?'

'*Sir* Thomas Sapsea,' came the reply, with a slight note of dignified reproach. 'The Crown, with that bounteous graciousness which is ever the hallmark and delight of our Constitution (and the envy of foreigners of every race and clime), saw fit to reward its most humble of servants, some years ago, for some modest functions performed in a civic, in a mayoral capacity, for this insignificant little community of ours. They also serve, gentlemen, however lowly their grade in life – they also serve,' and a hand was waved in deprecatory fashion, as a means of emphasizing that, whatever the insignificance of his achievements in the great scheme of things, the Cloisterham that we saw about us was largely the creation of his labours.

'You are too good,' he said, smilingly, with a further deprecatory wave of the hand, after we had conveyed our congratulations, 'you are far too good. But may I take this opportunity, gentlemen, as a senior citizen of our small town (and some, indeed, have been so kind as to refer to me as the permanent *first* citizen, an unmerited accolade which I totally, nay absolutely, reject), may I take this opportunity of welcoming you to Cloisterham and trusting that your visit is proving to be all that you could wish it to be? Is everything, in short, to your satisfaction, gentlemen?' – with an air of one who would most definitely take it upon himself to personally seek out, reprimand, chastise and generally demolish any wretched denizen who had in any way, however unwittingly, crossed our path.

'A charming city,' said Holmes. 'One could wish, perhaps, that accommodation for passing visitors were in greater supply, for The Crozier is fully booked up, but we are lodging with Mr and Mrs Tope and they have made us more than welcome.'

'A worthy couple,' said Sir Thomas, magnanimously.

'My friend and I', added Holmes, 'are considering the possibility, indeed, of acquiring a small residence in this fair city, as a place of retreat at such times of the year as the present, and have been casting our eyes on one or two properties that appear to be in a vacant or semi-vacant condition. As the leading expert on valuation and property in this part of the world, Sir Thomas, what would you say about the possibility of such an apartment as *that*' – and he pointed to the gatehouse – 'becoming available at a modest price?'

'That particular property', said Sir Thomas, with a shake of the head,' is not on the market, gentlemen. It is the residence of Mr John Jasper.'

Holmes looked mildly surprised. 'I had the impression', he said, 'that it was unoccupied.'

'At the moment, sir, I fear that it is. My friend Mr John Jasper, sir, has been gone from Cloisterham for many a long day,' he intoned. 'For many a long day,' he repeated with emphasis. 'But I cherish the hope that he will one day return to us.'

'Ah!' said Holmes, as though an old recollection had struck him. 'Is this the gentleman whose nephew suddenly disappeared?' A portentous nod greeted this question. 'And there was some talk, was there not, of another young gentleman, a Mr Landless, being responsible?'

'A bad lot, sir, a thoroughly bad lot!' – and a contemptuous snap of the fingers as though to say 'There! I totally dismiss him.'

'And Mr Jasper, therefore . . .?'

'Went in pursuit of the Murderer, gentlemen, and pledged himself never to rest easy in his bed until he had brought him to justice.'

Holmes shook his head in mournful reflection on the evils of the world.

'I am impressed to learn, gentlemen,' continued Sir Thomas, 'that the events of our small community should have made themselves known to the outside world and been so long remembered in . . . in circles such as your own.'

This last in slightly questioning vein.

'We must look elsewhere for a residence,' said Holmes ruefully, ignoring the hint. 'But I must confess that the city of Cloisterham greatly appeals to us.'

'Its peace and stillness', I added in an unlucky moment, feeling that it was time I made a further contribution to the discussion, 'certainly provide a welcome contrast to the hustle and bustle of Baker Street.'

'Of Baker Street?' repeated the old gentleman with unexpected alacrity, his eyes opening wide and gazing at Holmes with newly awakened interest. 'And fully conversant with the disappearance of Mr John Jasper's nephew, Mr Edwin Drood! Have I the honour of speaking to one who is professionally involved in criminological matters? Is it a Celebrated Sleuth that I see before me?'

Holmes, who had darted a look of intense irritation at myself, spread wide his hands with the air of one who, hopelessly outmatched, judged it best to surrender without further ado. 'Sir Thomas,' he said, 'you are far too deep for us. It is useless to conceal my identity so far as you are concerned. But you will appreciate, Sir Thomas, that my colleague and I are visiting Cloisterham in a strictly private capacity, as a break from the turmoils of London, and it would be greatly appreciated if you would preserve our secret.'

Sir Thomas tapped his nose in knowing fashion. 'Gentlemen,' he declared, manfully suppressing his excitement, 'you may rely upon me. I am the soul of discretion. Upon my word, a Celebrated Sleuth in Cloisterham! I must now take leave of you but I hope that we shall have the opportunity for further converse and I trust, again, that your stay proves a pleasant one. Once more, the compliments of the festive season!'

'Sir Thomas,' said Holmes, 'we are forever in your debt — and not least, I must add, for the inspiring sentiments with which you have enlivened our morning,' with a gesture towards the churchyard.

The venerable first citizen of Cloisterham vigorously shook his head. 'A poor thing, gentlemen,' he declared, 'a poor thing, but mine own!' And he took his leave. I was not at all clear, in my own mind, whether he was referring to the inscription on the tomb or to the late lamented Mrs Sapsea.

'I fancy', said my companion drily, 'that our presence here will be known throughout the streets of Cloisterham by the time the Cathedral clock strikes twelve. Of Baker Street, indeed! But here, Watson, is what I noted earlier this morning.' Holmes pointed through the railing at one particular headstone. SACRED TO THE MEMORY, it ran, OF MARTIN DROOD, DEPARTED THIS LIFE 14 MARCH 1861.

'Well, that certainly confirms,' I remarked, albeit not greatly impressed, 'quite apart from the remarks of Sir Thomas, that there is some tangible basis for Mr Jasper's story.'

'Think, man, think!'

I looked again and enlightenment dawned. 'Good heavens, Holmes! Of course, that date is quite impossible!'

'Exactly. Martin Drood was a gentleman of some technical ingenuity, I gather, and the genetic sciences have made great strides in recent years, but I fail to understand how even he could have fathered, twelve years prior to the year 1861, a son who would not come of age until the spring of 1894.'

'But this makes nonsense of virtually everything Mr Jasper told us! Are we the victims, Holmes, of some monstrous practical joke?'

'I doubt it. Mr Jasper, whatever else he may be, is no practical joker. The humour of our quandary escapes me and even the late Professor Moriarty, I fancy, would not have thought it worth his while to send us on a wild-goose chase to this inoffensive little town. No, there is nothing at all comic in the situation – just the reverse. The story that this Mr Jasper told us was narrated, I believe, in good faith and we have had the independent corroboration of Sir Thomas Sapsea on that score.' He paused for a moment, in some slight embarrassment. 'I fancy, Watson, that you will not believe me when I say that I half expected some development of this kind, or even if I add that it tends to clarify rather than obscure matters?'

'I know better than to doubt your word after all these years, Holmes, but I must certainly confess that I am totally bewildered.'

'Let us take a turn in the cloisters. This path is becoming rather too well frequented and I have no desire to draw undue attention to ourselves or to attract the conversation of another Sir Thomas Sapsea, if such there be! The morning service will be commencing shortly, and seclusion is required if we are to put our thoughts in order.'

The stream of pedestrians, of good-humoured families of all ages and sizes muffled up and chattering happily as they converged upon the Cathedral, was indeed growing

55

formidable. We strolled into the precincts, gently illuminated by wintry sunshine and as deserted as one could wish,
and perambulated them in silence for a time.

'You will recall', said Holmes at length, 'that I asked Mr
Jasper several questions towards the end of our interview
and that he was unable to enlighten me as to either the
frequency of the rail service or, as it transpires, the identity
of the present landlord of The Crozier. He acknowledged
that Christmas Eve was upon us, but I did not think to ask
him – indeed, I could scarcely have ventured to do so, even
had the thought occurred to me! – what year of Our Lord he
thought we were in. Had I done so, and had he retained
sufficient control of his temper to answer a singular but
simple question in a straightforward manner, I now suspect
that he would have opted for 1870 rather than 1894. By this
reckoning, Edwin Drood disappeared at midnight on the
Christmas Eve of 1869 and we are investigating an event
that occurred a quarter of a century ago. Our client's letter,
of course, was correctly dated but you will recall that the
date was inserted in another hand.'

I digested this information, shaking my head in
wonderment.

'The trains, of course, did not run to Cloisterham until
after 1870 and I feel certain that mine host at The Crozier in
that year (and some elementary research will soon confirm
this) would indeed have been Mr Bastewell.' He paused.
'What should instantly have alerted me to the strangeness
of Mr Jasper's narrative – and, indeed, suspicions were
slowly dawning that all was not right with it from the
chronological viewpoint – was his reference to Mehemet

Ali. The Levantine crisis that he referred to occurred in 1840, or thereabouts, which means that Mr Martin Drood and his wife would have arrived in Egypt in, say, 1845. You will recall that visit I paid to Great George Street yesterday morning. I was hoping that the Institution of Civil Engineers would be able to enlighten me as to the professional qualifications and career of one or other of the Droods, but I drew a blank on both counts. It simply did not occur to me to go further back into the records.'

'So Mr Jasper is suffering from some kind of amnesia?'

'We are now venturing into what are more properly *your* realms rather than mine, Watson, but that would certainly appear to be the case. A most curious kind of affliction, however: while convinced, as I take it, that he was talking to us on the twenty-third day of December in the year 1870, he had nevertheless been able to keep abreast of certain current events — being particularly (and flatteringly!) familiar, it seems, with the events of my own recent career.'

'But where is Mr Jasper now, Holmes? And, even more to the point, what do we do next?'

I realized, at this point, that Holmes had steered us out of the cloisters and that we were now approaching, once again, our curious lodgings.

'Do, my boy?' he exclaimed, with a positive hint of glee. 'There is only one course open to us on this beautiful Christmas morning. While the good people of Cloisterham are at their devotions a little breaking and entry on the part of a pair of old reprobates such as ourselves will surely not come amiss. Cometh the hour, cometh the intruders!' And he raised his stick and pointed at Jasper's gatehouse.

7

So, once again (and, as it proved, for the last time) we climbed that dusty postern staircase. Such daylight as could penetrate to the steps made it clear, had we still been in any doubt, that no feet but ours had trod them in recent months.

It took Holmes little more than five minutes' careful probing at the lock, with a curious instrument which he invariably carried on his person (akin, perhaps, to a remarkable penknife but with attachments that would have been the envy of any schoolboy), to secure our admission to the music-master's chambers. We found ourselves in a large room with two latticed windows directly opposite one another, the first overlooking the High Street and the second gazing towards the Cathedral and its precincts. It was an impressive, respectably furnished room – the abode, obviously, of an erudite man – with a pair of comfortable easy chairs on each side of the fireplace, a wall lined with shelves of books, a grand piano in a recess (although how *it* could have gained access to the upper storey of the gatehouse defied all rational analysis!) and a music stand, with one or two folios still on it. But dust was everywhere and the atmosphere was stale and musty in the extreme. One's initial inclination, which had to be restrained for obvious reasons, was to fling open wide the windows.

'Undoubtedly,' said Holmes, 'this is the residence of Mr John Jasper, although I should not like to hazard a guess, for the moment, as to when he last resided here.' His attention was caught by what was, perhaps, the one human touch in the room – a painting, which hung over the fireplace, of a pretty young girl with long brown hair streaming down to her shoulders and an impertinent twinkle in her eyes. It was amateurishly executed and apparently unfinished but succeeded in conveying a captivating impression of the young lady's character. It roguishly enlivened what was otherwise a rather solemn bachelor apartment. 'A striking young lady,' said Holmes. 'And that brooch she wears is equally striking' – he pointed to an amethyst in a gold setting of peculiar intricacy, designed to resemble a budding rose. 'That may give us a clue', he added with a smile, 'as to the identity of the young person!'

A small dining-room lay beyond this austere chamber with a door at the far end (leading, we surmised, to the quarters of Mr and Mrs Tope). Holmes poked and probed around both rooms without finding anything of interest and then led the way up a short flight of steps to two modestly-sized bedrooms. The smaller of them appeared to be principally for guests, there being nothing of a personal nature in the wardrobe or chest of drawers, but the main bedroom, which was clearly Mr Jasper's own, was more rewarding. 'See here!' exclaimed Holmes, holding aloft (after blowing the dust away) a notebook which he had found on the bedside table. 'This appears to be some kind of diary kept by our client – and, yes, the entries relate to events in 1869 and 1870! Look at these, Watson – both written in September 1869.'

The first entry ran as follows:

Past midnight. – After what I have just now seen, I have a morbid dread upon me of some horrible consequences resulting to my dear boy, that I cannot reason with or in any way contend against. All my efforts are vain. The demoniacal passion of this Neville Landless, his strength in his fury, and his savage rage for the destruction of its object, appal me. So profound is the impression, that twice since I have gone into my dear boy's room, to assure myself of his sleeping safely, and not lying dead in his blood.

And the second, written the following morning:

Ned up and away. Light-hearted and unsuspicious as ever. He laughed when I cautioned him, and said he was as good a man as Neville Landless any day. I told him that he might be, but he was not so bad a man. He continued to make light of it, but I travelled with him as far as I could, and left him most unwillingly. I am unable to shake off these dark intangible presentiments of evil – if feelings founded upon staring facts are to be so called.

I shivered. 'Poor Mr Jasper', I said, 'had full justification for his terrible forebodings. He seems, indeed, to have been virtually clairvoyant! Neville Landless must surely have

60

behaved like some kind of uncaged wild beast, on the occasion of his first visit to the gatehouse, to have aroused such apprehensions on the part of our client.'

'I certainly agree', replied Holmes, 'that he was finely attuned to the tension between these two young men. The quarrel between them, you will recall, concerned Miss Bud, and on such a subject as a member of the fairer sex passions can be aroused to an alarming degree. But what have we here? A letter from Mr Drood himself, it seems, written at the beginning of December 1869!'

The letter in question, which had been folded up and inserted in the diary, ran as follows:

My Dear Jack,

I am touched by your account of your interview with Mr Crisparkle, whom I much respect and esteem. At once I openly say that I forgot myself on that occasion quite as much as Mr Landless did, and that I wish that bygone to be a bygone, and all to be right again.

Look here, dear old boy. Ask Mr Landless to dinner on Christmas Eve (the better the day the better the deed), and let there be only we three, and let us shake hands all round there and then, and say no more about it.

My dear Jack, Ever your most affectionate,
Edwin Drood

P.S. Love to Miss Pussy at the next music-lesson.

'A frank, impetuous, good-hearted youth!' I exclaimed. 'His character emerges very clearly from this letter, and from the second of those two diary entries. One can fully see why Mr Jasper was so fond of him. And the young man appears to have been equally fond of his uncle.'

'Miss Pussy', said Holmes, somewhat drily, 'is presumably Miss Bud. That young lady evidently has a significant part to play in this tale. So, the stage is set for that fateful meeting on Christmas Eve 1869. What else does the diary have to tell us?'

There were a number of blank pages and then came a further entry, penned towards the end of January 1870:

My dear boy is murdered. The discovery of the watch and shirt-pin convinces me that he was murdered that night, and that his jewellery was taken from him to prevent identification by its means. All the delusive hopes I had founded on his separation from his betrothed wife, I give to the winds. They perish before this fatal discovery. I now swear, and record the oath on this page, that I nevermore will discuss this mystery with any human creature until I hold the clue to it in my hand. That I never will relax in my secrecy or in my search. That I will fasten the crime of the murder of my dear dead boy upon the murderer. And, that I devote myself to his destruction.

'It appears', I said, 'that Mr Jasper broke his oath when he came to see us.'

'Unless', said Holmes, musingly, 'the day *did* come when he held the clue to the mystery in his hand. But perhaps he regards me — not altogether flatteringly, it must be confessed! — as being in a category one stage removed from the ordinary human creature. He was also, of course, far less emphatic, both in his letter to me and in our conversation, as to the ultimate fate of Mr Drood. The man who wrote this diary entry had no doubts whatsoever on the subject; the man we saw two days ago desperately wanted to know, simply for his own peace of mind, whether Drood was alive or dead. That suggests that something happened, prior to his memory playing strange tricks with him, to shake Mr Jasper's certainty on the matter.'

'But these diary entries (and, of course, Mr Drood's letter)', I pointed out, 'amply confirm your conjecture that these are events which happened a quarter of a century ago. Is there really any point in our further involvement in what could almost be classed as ancient history?'

'These documents are certainly extremely convenient,' Holmes agreed. 'So convenient, indeed, as to suggest that we — or somebody else — had positively been *intended* to see them. But there is a mystery here, Watson, irrespective of whether it happened yesterday, twelve months ago or twenty-five years ago, and I think we need to penetrate a little deeper before washing our hands of the affair. Does this diary have anything more to tell us? Ah, see here!'

He had been turning the blank pages of the volume and came to a halt at two entries written on consecutive days at the beginning of July. The first ran as follows:

I have said what I had to say to Rosa. I could not help myself. I have laid my all before her and I have warned her of the consequences of rejection.

And the second:

> I am spurned. The bird has flown the nest. I warned her of
> the consequences! So be it.

'There is', observed Holmes, 'a positively threatening
note about these later entries – written, you will observe, in
a larger hand than before. I am not at all sure that we were
intended to see *them*! Is there anything further, I wonder?'

He continued to turn the pages, which had reverted to
the status of blank sheets, and it was not until he approached
the end of the year 1870 that two further entries appeared.
The first, written on 23 December, ran as follows:

> Rosa is to marry another! So much for her devotion to the
> memory of my dear boy. Mr Grewgious, whose attitude
> towards me during recent months has been abrupt to the
> point of rudeness, positively sought me out today, after
> calling on Miss Twinkleton, to tell me what he described
> as the glad tidings. And poor Ned, this time last year, was
> so close to winning her! – closer, now, than I had ever
> appreciated before.

And the second:

> A year ago today that Ned disappeared. But I have a
> curious feeling upon me that retribution is at hand and
> that the Murderer, at long last, is to be revealed. The
> Lord's will be done!

There were no further entries.

'So matters came to a head, it seems, on the Christmas

Eve of 1870,' said Holmes, closing the book. 'In what way, I wonder? And what could it have been that Mr Jasper learnt about his nephew from Mr Grewgious that he had not been aware of before?'

He stood there, absorbed in conjecture for some minutes, before shaking his head. 'It is futile', he said, 'to engage in speculation in the absence of sufficient data. But the other point of interest to emerge from these entries is that Mr Jasper, with his nephew out of the running, apparently offered himself to Miss Bud as an alternative suitor and was soundly rejected for his pains.'

'A grotesque idea!' I exclaimed.

'Not necessarily. We need, of course, to re-orientate our thoughts on this affair now that we know of the passage of twenty-five years. Mr Jasper, when we saw him two days ago, was a haggard gentleman with greyish hair. When due allowance has been made for the anxieties that he has undergone (and also, for that matter, a certain type of medication that I suspect him to have been indulging in), I would judge him to be in his early fifties. It appeared perfectly reasonable to us that a middle-aged gentleman should be concerned about the disappearance of a nephew aged no more than twenty. He referred to him then, and he refers to him in this diary, as his "dear boy", yet at the time Edwin Drood disappeared he himself could surely not have been more than twenty-seven or twenty-eight – perhaps even younger. If there were, say, an age difference of no more than six or seven years between them then a rather different picture begins to emerge. They would have been more like brothers than uncle and nephew.'

'Then the difference in age between Mr Jasper and his sister must have been substantial?'

Holmes nodded. 'It is time, I think, that we put some provisional dates to the sequence of events. Elizabeth Jasper married Martin Drood in, let us say, 1847 – almost six years after the Levantine crisis – and Edwin, destined to come of age in 1870, was born in 1849. John Jasper would have been born in 1843 or therabouts, being some fifteen years younger than his sister. Elizabeth dies soon after the birth of Edwin. Father and son then return to England, where they settle down in Cloisterham, in close proximity to the elder Jaspers. In the meantime, Miss Bud would have been born in 1853 – for she is four years Edwin's junior, you will recall – and her father, Martin's dearest friend, dies in 1860. Martin himself dies in 1861. Mr and Mrs Jasper die sometime in the mid-1860s and John becomes Edwin's guardian. We are now, I think, fully apprised of all we need to know of the immediate historical background.'

'So Miss Bud, by this reckoning, would be only ten years younger than John Jasper.'

'Quite. But the prospect of their being united in matrimony obviously did not appeal to her, despite a mysterious threat that he apparently coupled with his proposal, and she instantly fled to London – to take refuge, presumably, with Mr Grewgious. But what have we *here?*'

Holmes had been casting a speculative eye over the contents of the bedroom all the time that he had been speaking. Plunging a hand into the inner recesses of a bedside locker he now brought to light, with a cry of triumph, a small pipe of rather curious design. 'You will recall, Watson,' he remarked with a smile, 'that I thought that I had once encountered Mr Jasper on a previous occasion under rather strange circumstances — this little item may give you some inkling of what those circumstances were. But no more of that, for the present!'

He carefully replaced the pipe in the locker and led the way down the short flight of stairs. On the way, however, his attention was caught by a slight protuberance from the medieval wall, a foot or so above his head. He paused for a moment, felt over the area with singular intentness and then gave the protuberance a wrench. The brick in question, after a brief resistance, came away in his hand and he placed it carefully on one of the steps and then rummaged in the small cavity that it had left behind. Again, a cry of triumph as he brought to light a very large, very rusty, and very heavy metal key. 'Now what could *this* be?' he mused. 'I have the feeling, Watson, that if we could only find the door that this key unlocks we might be materially advanced in our quest.' He weighed it in his hand, frowning.

'Now *that* surely is pure fancy, Holmes!'

'You are quite right, of course, and yet it puzzles me. Far too big for a safe, but not the normal kind of key for the normal kind of door. And why, in any case, should it be hidden?' He replaced it in the cavity and restored the stone, shaking his head in perplexity.

'For safekeeping, obviously.'

'But Mr Jasper is the only person who lived in these chambers. From whom should he wish to hide it?'

We had returned, by this time, to the main apartment and I was about to answer Holmes (although, for the life of me, I cannot now recall what I was going to say) when we were disturbed by a slight sound. Turning, we found that Mrs Tope, framed in the distant doorway, was gazing at us with astonishment from the tiny dining-room.

8

'Do not be alarmed, Mrs Tope!' called out Holmes reassuringly, for the good lady was obviously much distressed. 'As I explained to your husband last night, we are friends of Mr Jasper and had arranged to call on him. Since he is not in residence, rather to our surprise and concern, we had hoped that we might discover some clue as to his whereabouts.'

'But he's not been here for years, gentlemen!' cried an amazed Mrs Tope. 'Not for years and years. And you're friends of his, you say?'

'Acquaintances, perhaps, would be a more accurate description. Yes, we met him two days ago and it was agreed that we should visit him without delay. It had not occurred to us, obviously, that we would not find him at home.'

Mrs Tope shook her head in wonderment. 'But how did you get in?' she asked. 'Did Mr Jasper give you a key? And how is he? How does the poor man look?'

We explained that, yes, we did have a key to the chambers, that Mr Jasper had seemed reasonably well, apart from shortness of breath and a shaking hand, but that he was much concerned about the fate of his nephew and had sought our advice on this matter.

'After all these years!' exclaimed Mrs Tope. 'The good man always was too much wrapped up in Master Edwin — he was that worried about him, you would scarcely credit.' She had recovered, by this time, most of her composure and suggested that we might like to accompany her back to the Tope quarters to partake of (yet another) nice cup of tea, an invitation which we thought it politic to accept.

'But I wonder, Mrs Tope,' said Holmes, just as we were on the point of leaving Mr Jasper's apartment, 'whether you could perhaps enlighten us as to the identity of the young lady in the picture over there? Would one be right in assuming that it was a portrait of Miss Rosa Bud?'

Mrs Tope confirmed that our supposition was correct and added that it had been painted by Master Edwin. She explained, as she led the way through to the Topes' own modest living-room on the far side of the gatehouse, that she had been accustomed to play the role of housekeeper to Mr Jasper, when he was in residence, and that since it was at a Christmas time that he had left Cloisterham very suddenly, many years before, there had never been a Christmas since when she had not half expected his reappearance — and hearing the sound of voices, on her return from morning service, she had excitedly jumped to the conclusion that the long-awaited event had finally come about.

'You miss him, then?' asked Holmes sympathetically.

'Ah, he was that good a gentleman, sirs, and so much

70

worry to bear – and the choir, it's said, has never sung nowhere near as good since he left!'

We were seated, at this time, round a small table while Mrs Tope did the honours with her teapot and here we were joined, a few minutes later, by her husband, his Christmas Day duties as verger now fully discharged. He joined in the ensuing conversation from time to time, although evidently hard of hearing (as we had suspected the previous evening), and we learnt virtually all that they had to tell us on the subject of Mr Jasper. That his music, and his concern for his nephew's welfare, were his two consuming passions – although there had been a time, thought Mr Tope, when he had contemplated writing a history of the Cathedral, being jovially accused by the Dean (no less) of intending to put them all in a book, and to this end had accompanied the then stonemason (a Mr Durdles, long since deceased) on a midnight tour of the crypt and the cloisters and goodness knows what else. That the disappearance of Master Edwin, in mighty suspicious circumstances, had come close to unhinging him. That he had regained control of himself and resumed his activities in the local community to some extent, although wounded, perhaps, by the manner in which one or two folk who ought to have known better had seemingly turned against him. That Miss Bud, whose talents as a singer he had spent many long hours assiduously cultivating, and who might have been expected to be especially sympathetic to him in view of the great loss they had both shared, had abruptly terminated her musical studies and flounced off to London. That Mr Jasper himself had gone away suddenly on a Christmas Eve, exactly a year

71

after the day on which his nephew disappeared. That there was a strong school of thought (exemplified, as we were already aware, by Sir Thomas Sapsea) which understood him to be pursuing the Murderer and was thoroughly convinced that he would never return to Cloisterham until the villain had been brought to justice. That it was not clear how or where this theory had originated, except that it seemed to fit the known facts. That nothing more had been heard of him, from that day to this, except on two rather curious occasions – occasions, indeed, oddly akin to our own visitation, for both had involved a pair of gentlemen not altogether dissimilar from ourselves.

'Indeed!' said Holmes. 'Perhaps you can tell me more?'

'The first time', said Mrs Tope, 'was some three years after Mr Jasper went. These two gentlemen called, bearing a note signed by himself, which gave them authorization to fetch away some of his books and his writing paper.'

'And why could Mr Jasper not call in person for these items?'

'They said he was . . .' There was much intense concentration on Mrs Tope's part, as she struggled to recall the elusive word.

'"Indisposed,"' put in her consort, gruffly.

'That's it, gentlemen! "Indisposed",' said Mrs Tope in triumphant relief.

'And the second occasion?'

'This would be some ten or twelve years back. Two gentlemen arrived who said, like yourselves, that they were looking for him and wondered whether he had been home recently. They said that they were friends of his but had temporarily lost touch with him.'

'But you were unable to help them?'

Confirmation from Mrs Tope.

'And were they the same two gentlemen who had called previously?'

One of them, she thought, might be (although she was not prepared to swear to this) but the other had been unfamiliar. On the subject of Master Edwin's disappearance, neither she nor her husband was able to tell us anything that we had not learnt already from Mr Jasper. Questioned about Mr Neville Landless, she recalled him as a rather wild, headstrong person who, even before the disappearance of Mr Drood, had been regarded with a certain degree of aversion in the town. And as for *after* the disappearance, the good lady's indignation was scarcely strong enough to contain itself. That such a man should have been allowed to walk the streets was nothing short of a public disgrace! His guardian, Mr Crisparkle, had spirited him away to London as soon as he had been officially cleared, in the absence of any positive evidence, of having committed a crime, and just as well it was too!

'And Mr Landless never returned to Cloisterham?'

'No, *he* never came back, although of course –'

But at this point Mrs Tope was vigorously cautioned by her husband to say no more on the subject of Mr Landless or anything pertaining to him. 'There are certain matters, gentlemen,' he sternly advised us, 'that is best left undisturbed. London looks after its own, gentlemen, and Cloisterham does likewise.'

There being, by this time, a certain restlessness on Mr

Tope's part, which had evinced itself even before these final enigmatic utterances, we thought it best to bring the interview to a close, to thank them warmly for the tea and information, and return to our own quarters. 'So Mr Jasper', said Holmes thoughtfully, 'has had encounters with two gentlemen of a vaguely officious character on more than one occasion, which suggests that he was not altogether surprised by the events of the other evening – resentful, yes, but seemingly resigned (as I recall it) to his fate. Does that suggest anything to you, Watson? And what, I wonder, was the item of information relating to Mr Landless which Mrs Tope was about to impart? No matter – we are sure to learn it from some other source. Of more immediate concern, I would suggest, is the fact that it is now one o'clock. I propose that we call once more at The Crozier to see what further delights Mr Appleby can offer us in the way of festive fare.'

But, before we could set out, there came a tap at the door and our landlady ushered in a breathless small boy. He pipingly announced that he had come post-haste from the Deanery with a message to the effect that the Dean and his family would be greatly honoured if the two gentlemen visitors currently staying at the Tope residence would care to join the said Dean and said family for lunch in about one hour's time. 'The first citizen of Cloisterham', murmured Holmes to me, 'has, I fancy, been at work here' but to the youthful messenger he conveyed the tidings (simultaneously pressing a shilling into the small palm) that the two gentlemen would be delighted to avail themselves of the kind and unexpected invitation.

Our credentials of respectability fully restored, as it were, in the eyes of Mrs Tope (for I had been unable to rid myself of the uneasy feeling, cups of tea and sundry confidences notwithstanding, that we had rather fallen from grace after being discovered in the Jasper apartment) we sallied forth to our Christmas lunch at the Deanery.

9

Pangs of conscience, however, also smote me when we arrived at the Deanery, a substantial red-brick residence of the Queen Anne period, for I was struck by the sudden realization that, unlike Holmes, I had not set foot in the Cathedral that morning (except in the earliest of hours) and yet here I was, on this day of all days, accepting clerical hospitality at the highest level. Trusting, however, that my absence from the two morning services would not have been remarked upon, I accompanied Holmes into the spacious Deanery and found our new surroundings a welcome relief after the claustrophobic atmosphere of the gatehouse.

A maid, relieving us of our coats, showed us into the drawing-room and here we waited while our arrival was announced to the master of the house. The distant sounds of high-spirited laughter came to our ears, indicating that younger folk were in evidence, and Holmes, in relaxed mood, strolled round the room studying the furniture and a small gallery of portraits. What took his fancy, in the first instance, was a massive sideboard of curious design. 'I have not seen one of those', he remarked, 'since my childhood, but I remember it well. An ingenious idea, Watson: only one section can be opened at a time, the top half of the cabinet being completely unaware, as it were, of the bottom half's existence.'

We cast our eyes over the portraits. One of them, which dominated the room, was of a very striking, dark-haired young woman, slim and tall with stern, belligerent eyes, which virtually challenged the onlooker (or, for that matter, the world in general) to cross swords with her if he (or it) dared. There was a smouldering intensity about the figure which the artist had captured with remarkable adroitness. The characteristics of her face were reflected, to some extent, in a small head-and-shoulders sketch of a young man which hung a short distance away, except that *his* expression was of a more melancholy, brooding kind: one felt that *he* had wearied of fighting battles, and simply waited for the end. The third portrait was far different again, being that of a sweet, dimpled old lady, who gazed at us half in welcoming pleasure and half in warning admonition.

'My mother, gentlemen,' came a voice from our left, as the Dean entered the room. 'The dearest of souls, but the sternest of taskmasters! God rest her soul. Gentlemen, I am heartily glad that you are able to join us for Christmas lunch. Welcome to Cloisterham, Mr Sexton Blake!'

Holmes, unable to help himself, let out a loud whoop of delight which he endeavoured, totally without success, to convert into a cough. While he spluttered and, indeed, almost choked in his merriment, I endeavoured to explain to our puzzled and embarrassed host that there had been something of a misunderstanding and that Sexton Blake was a fictional creation who had recently begun to appear in the crudest of cheap magazine papers – a character based, admittedly, upon that of my friend, even to the extent of residing in Baker Street, but a shocking travesty of the original.

The poor Dean hastened to make amends for his mistake. 'A thousand pardons, gentlemen,' he exclaimed. 'You must appreciate that we in Cloisterham, though relatively close to London, are woefully behind the times in our awareness of current events and personalities in the great city. It was Sir Thomas Sapsea who informed me, in tremendous excitement, that a personage no less important than Sexton Blake himself had arrived in our little town and that Cloisterham was being shockingly remiss in offering him and his companion adequate hospitality. The name was slightly familiar to me but your own, I must confess, is even more portentous! You really must forgive us for our stupidity, Mr Holmes. We lead a sheltered existence, and that is all I can say.'

'There is nothing to forgive, I do assure you,' Holmes managed, at length, to reply. 'It is I who should be apologizing for my mirth, which is disgracefully remiss, but the sheer delight of your unexpected greeting caught me totally unprepared! This is a salutary reminder of the vulnerability of those with allegedly well-established reputations when they venture into foreign climes. It confirms a theme which I was developing last night in conversation with my friend Dr Watson here, that the dividing line between fact and fiction is one that is blurred with increasing frequency in this day and age, even in the best regulated circles. I only hope, Dean, that you will not consider me guilty of accepting your hospitality under false pretences.'

The Dean assured us, with a hearty laugh, that he would most certainly harbour no such suspicion and, to demonstrate that his word was his bond, promptly opened up the top half of the sideboard in search of aperitifs. He was a large, good-tempered gentleman whose receding grey hair led me to conclude that he must be in his early sixties. His open, ruddy complexion rendered him, however, the picture of health and he gave the general impression of being much younger than his years. Conviviality firmly established, he beamingly shepherded us into the dining-room and introduced us to his wife and family and fellow-guests (among whom, I was pleased to note, Sir Thomas did *not* feature). His wife, some fifteen years younger than himself, was instantly recognizable as the original of the young woman in the drawing-room portrait. Her dark hair had now become silver and her eyes had lost, perhaps, something of their fire, but her overall demeanour was that of someone who was relaxed and generally content. She welcomed us warmly and declared (when the misunderstanding had been explained) that *she* was perfectly capable of distinguishing between the genuine and counterfeit Sleuths of Baker Street and had been convinced from the outset that Sir Thomas had been gloriously confused. She then rushed away to supervise operations in the kitchen, from which promising aromas were emanating.

The absurd confusion over Holmes's own identity had

put a curb on the social niceties in the opposite direction, for the Dean had not had an opportunity to introduce himself formally and the longer we were there the more impossible it became to enquire his name. Holmes, however, was evidently unaware of any such problem, and simply addressed our host as 'Dean' and his wife as 'ma'am'. I followed suit, but when the time came for us to be introduced to the junior members of the household – a high-spirited lad in his early twenties and two young ladies who were, it transpired, still attending the Nuns' House seminary (the current principal of which, Mrs Tisher, was one of the guests) – my heart missed a beat, for the name of the young man was Neville and his sisters were called Helen and Rose. I began, at that point, to have a very strong inkling as to the name of our host (who was addressed, by his wife, as 'Septimus'), and the identity of the gloomy young man in the sketch, who bore an uncanny resemblance to the son of the house, was a mystery no longer.

The Christmas dinner was all that one could have desired and I flatter myself that we needed little encouragement to fall to and do it ample justice in the time-honoured tradition. A splendid goose, with all the trimmings, speedily came and went and an impressive plum pudding suffered a similar fate (although we were informed that its twin, equally impressive, was ready to take its place if the need should arise).

'So, Mr Holmes,' said the Dean at length, pushing back his plate, 'I gather that you contemplate taking up residence in Cloisterham at such time as you retire – or is it simply a holiday retreat that you have in mind?'

Holmes confessed, a trifle awkwardly, that the idea of

taking up residence in this pleasant little town had indeed crossed his mind. 'For the ambience', said he, 'is agreeable – as, too, are the residents – and the country air comes as a welcome relief after the fumes of London. But I believe that I am not the first fugitive from the great wen to have had this idea – there was a Mr Datchery here before me, was there not?'

'Old Dick Datchery!' said the Dean with a surprised smile. 'I haven't thought about him in years – fancy you knowing about old Dick! Yes, you're quite right, he too came to Cloisterham to retire – and he lived in the very same lodgings as those in which you and Dr Watson spent last night. Quite a character, in his way – a retired old buffer of independent means, or so he described himself, and that was all we ever learnt about him. Sir Thomas – or *Mr* Sapsea, as he then was – was convinced that he had been something to do with the diplomatic service, but I fancy old Dick was pulling his leg. Yes, he took to Cloisterham like a duck to water during the short time that he was here. You remember him too, don't you, my dear?'

Mrs Dean regretted that, for various reasons (and a shadow crossed her face as she spoke), she had been obliged to be elsewhere during the period in question.

'Of course, of course,' said the Dean hastily, resuming at top speed (as though to put as much distance as he could between himself and some disagreeable recollections) his reminiscences of Dick Datchery. 'A funny old boy,' he continued, affectionately, 'but a real Christian gentleman. One often saw him strolling about the town, buttoned up in that tight blue surtout of his, talking to whomever took his fancy, totally regardless of who they were or where they came from. Old Durdles, the stonemason, was one person who appealed to him: they got on famously together, and take my word for it, there weren't many people for whom Durdles could spare more than a passing grunt! On another occasion I saw him helping a poor wreck of an incredibly dirty old woman on to the London coach (for that was before the trains came direct to Cloisterham) with as much solicitude as if she had been the Queen herself. I said as much to him afterwards. 'Mr Crisparkle,' said he, with twinkling eye, 'that lady, sir, is a genuine princess, take my word for it!"'

Holmes appeared to take a keen interest in these stories. 'You say, Dean,' he responded, 'that Mr Datchery was only here for a short time. Did he end his days in Cloisterham or did he move on to some other resting place?'

'The strange thing is,' said the Dean, 'that I really don't know what became of Mr Datchery. I never saw the coming of him and I never saw the going of him — one simply became aware that he was no longer with us, although I don't recall any farewells. A curious old gentleman, but one to whom I (and, for that matter, my wife, although she never met him — and, indeed, she had not then done me the honour of actually becoming my wife!) am much indebted for invaluable advice and assistance. There was something of a crisis in our affairs at that time, the details of which I will not pursue, and he played a considerable part in seeking to remedy matters. I will not say that he was wholly successful, but he was a good friend to us at a time when good friends were in rather short supply.'

The Dean's wife had been observing my colleague intently for some little while and now steered the conversation back to its original starting point. 'In looking for your ideal retirement home, Mr Holmes,' she said, with a slightly ironic note in her voice, 'did you alight upon Cloisterham purely by chance or was it recommended to you?'

'The truth of the matter, ma'am,' replied Holmes, in the most casual, agreeable of tones, toying with his glass as he spoke, 'is that we were invited here by a gentleman with whom you are no doubt acquainted – Mr John Jasper.'

This announcement came as a bombshell so far as Mr and Mrs Crisparkle and Mrs Tisher were concerned. The Dean's wife instantly went deathly white, Mrs Tisher dropped her spoon with a cry of horror and the Dean started back as though Banquo's ghost were advancing upon him. He swallowed for an instant and found some difficulty in speaking. All this while the three younger members of the family, evidently unaware of any cause for consternation, stared in amazement at their elders. It seemed, for a time, that the silence would never be broken.

'The gentleman you refer to', said the Dean at last, almost croaking the words, 'has not resided in Cloisterham for a very long while. I do not think that he will be returning to this city.' He helped himself to a glass of water and drank it down with shaking hand.

'When did you see this man?' demanded Mrs Crisparkle coldly – and she was, once again, the combative spirit whom the artist had depicted some twenty years before.

'Two days ago,' replied Holmes, seemingly unaware of

the sensation he had created. 'He called upon myself and Dr Watson and solicited our help in ascertaining what had become of his nephew, Mr Edwin Drood. We agreed to come down to Cloisterham without delay – unaware, of course, that he was referring to events which had taken place many years ago and totally unprepared for the fact that he would not be here to receive us.'

Again, the same stunned silence.

'And have you discovered anything?' asked Mrs Crisparkle at length, making no attempt to conceal the note of contempt in her voice.

'Some interesting items of information, certainly,' replied Holmes with equanimity, 'but I fancy that it will be some little while before I can formulate definite conclusions.'

The Dean's wife, livid with rage, rose and swept out of the room, much to the astonishment of her three children: the two girls hurried after her and the son stood up awkwardly, not comprehending the cause of this domestic upheaval but aware, obviously, that these two strangers were to blame for it and gazing at us with smouldering indignation. 'You must excuse my wife, gentlemen,' said poor Mr Crisparkle, doing his best to make amends. 'Helena is subject, at times, to the most appalling headaches. They overwhelm her without warning and she is obliged to instantly lie down on such occasions.'

We assured him that we totally understood and rose to take our leave. The conviviality of the dinner-table had now, alas, been totally destroyed and I was horrified at the effect that Holmes's announcement had had upon these good people. Their Christmas Day had evidently been ruined by our arrival on the scene and by this introduction of a spectre at the very conclusion of our feast. It seemed a poor return for their warm hospitality and I was consumed by far greater feelings of guilt than any others I had experienced that day.

The Dean's appeal to us to prolong our visit being politely declined (much to his evident relief) on the grounds that we must catch the five o'clock train to London, he saw us to the door. 'I appreciate, gentlemen,' he said, 'that you are strangers to this whole wretched Drood affair, that you are innocent parties, as it were, and have presumably come here with the best of intentions, but I really cannot wish you well of your investigations. What may be largely of academic interest to you, Mr Holmes, as something that happened many years ago and was never brought to a satisfactory conclusion, is an issue that is as alive, to other people, as though it happened yesterday. For twenty-four years we have lived here in peace. I feel that your probings can do nothing but harm and I beseech you to return to Baker Street and concern yourself with matters of more relevance to the present day and age.'

Holmes listened gravely to this appeal. 'I am sorry', he said, 'for the distress that I have evidently caused your wife and yourself but I can make no promises, Mr Crisparkle, about my future course of conduct. I hear what you say and I will give your sentiments my full consideration, but you must know that there is an allegiance I owe that must take precedence over all else.'

'To Mr Jasper, I suppose?'

'No, Mr Crisparkle, to Truth. Pray thank your wife for her

85

hospitality and I trust that she will soon be recovered from her indisposition. Once more, my apologies.'

We returned to the gatehouse. I said nothing, for I felt an overwhelming urge to escape from this little town where we had caused so much ill-feeling in so short a space of time, and Holmes for his part was sunk in thought. 'You will note', said he at length, 'that the Dean referred to a period of twenty-four years rather than one of twenty-five: the question of what happened on the Christmas Eve of 1870 is, obviously, as relevant to our investigation as what happened on the Christmas Eve of 1869.'

I returned what was, I fear, a rather brusque reply to this remark – for it was now abundantly clear that Holmes did indeed intend to pursue his enquiries – and busied myself with packing our bags while Holmes settled up our account with Mr and Mrs Tope.

It was at this point that I made the first of two curious discoveries. It had been dark when I stuffed our modest travelling accoutrements into the corner-cupboard the previous night and I had not appreciated the full extent to which it receded into the ancient stone wall. Stretching my hand deep into the middle section, in which the back of the shelf rather fell away from the front, I was startled to encounter what I took to be, at first, the remains of a cat or dog – for it was undoubtedly hair or fur of some description that my hand had fallen upon. Unpleasant though it was to the touch, I grasped the grim relic and brought it forth. To my astonishment, I found myself holding a very bedraggled, very dirty, very cobwebby mane of what had once been an abundance of white hair – in short, a wig. In dragging it out, however, I was aware of having disturbed something else. Plunging my hand back into the cupboard for a second time, and groping once more in its innermost depths, I now came up with something slightly stiffer and bulkier. This second item proved to be a hat. Within it was written, in faded ink, the name 'Datchery'.

'Excellent, Watson!' exclaimed Holmes, who had re-entered the room by this time and quietly come up behind me. 'Not for the first time, I am greatly indebted to you.' He held the hat between finger and thumb and examined it with great care, with the aid of his magnifying glass, by the fading light at the window. 'Seemingly worn', he remarked, 'by somebody with a very large head (in the same league, indeed, as that of Mr Henry Baker!), although the wig, when properly spruced up, would have accounted for most of its capacity. *Not* the type of headgear sold by the normal London hatters, but the remains of the label (apparently emanating from Messrs Bergstone and Ritchie, who once upon a time catered for thespians of all shapes and sizes) suggest, rather, that it would have been purchased in a theatrical costumier's. Some thirty or forty years back there was a vogue for rustic comedies on our stage and I suspect that it would then have adorned some village sage or yokel who would have been the prize performer of the evening. So far as the inscription is concerned, you will observe that the upper stroke of the 't' is in a darker ink than the rest of the name — it was evidently added as an afterthought. We must conclude, I think, that the gentleman who wore this battered headpiece did indeed contrive to free himself of the letter L.'

'And very fond of his tea,' I added, '– or could it have been the letter T?' For it was clear to me, now, that the old gentleman who had been Mrs Tope's last lodger could have been none other than Dick Datchery. I passed on to Holmes the information that the good lady had imparted to me earlier in the day, such as it was. He listened in silence, with the air of one not greatly surprised, and then stuffed the hat and wig into his bag. 'These may', he said, 'come in useful sometime. I doubt whether the original owner has any further need of them.'

We walked briskly to the station through the silent and increasingly chilly streets of Cloisterham, passing not a soul on the way, only to find that the five o'clock train was running some fifteen minutes late. I stamped up and down the platform to keep warm while Holmes engaged the burly porter in conversation. 'You must have seen', I heard him say, 'some remarkable changes since the railway came to Cloisterham.' I made no attempt to catch any more, for my irritation at Holmes's continuing interest in this affair – momentarily swept aside by the discovery of the Datchery wig and hat – had now renewed itself. It was impossible to forget the look of fury on Helena Crisparkle's face and the anguished appeal of the Dean, which had fallen, all too evidently, on unsympathtic ears.

Our near-empty train eventually arrived and we scrambled aboard, it being a relief to sink back into the seats. 'No stone, however seemingly insignificant, should be left unturned in an investigation of this kind,' said Holmes, who was (for once) in a more talkative mood than myself. 'That worthy custodian of the platform, a gentleman by the name of Joe, worked here as an omnibus driver in the days before the railway and was responsible for transporting Neville and Helena Landless into Cloisterham. He remembers the young man well and was, in fact, one of those who made up the party which apprehended him for the alleged murder of Edwin Drood on that Christmas morning of 1869. Landless resisted like a tiger, so he tells me, although our friend soon got the better of him. He also remembers Miss Rosa Bud ('the sweetest little lass in the town') and was responsible for transporting her *out* of Cloisterham some six months later. She was, it seems, in a state of great perturbation, as though the seven furies were pursuing her.' I wished, however, to hear no more about this affair and indicated as much by the shortness of my responses. Holmes, not one whit abashed, continued to muse aloud on what Joe had told him. 'I appreciate', he said at length, 'that you now have strong reservations, Watson, about our involvement in this case, and the Dean's appeal did not leave me wholly unmoved, but I fancy that we are at the midway point of our investigation. Having come so far, one might as well go on as turn back. Much has become clear, and yet certain crucial aspects remain in tantalizing, impenetrable darkness! If I can only pierce that veil, and clarify one or two outstanding matters to my own satisfaction, I am convinced that nothing but good can come of this investigation. The Crisparkle family, indeed, may even be the ultimate beneficiaries of our labours!'

I was mollified to some extent, although still inclined to the view that we were venturing into regions better left unexplored. And so, for the moment – for twelve whole months, in fact — we bade adieu to Cloisterham and the lights of the little town slipped away from us as the train gathered speed. 'I wonder', said Holmes dreamily, leaning back and composing himself for a nap, 'what Sexton Blake would have made of it all.'

10

My narrative has thus far been relatively straightforward,
being concerned solely with the Christmas of 1894 and the
events of three somewhat curious days. From this point
onwards it becomes, I fear, far more disjointed and I must
ask the reader to make every allowance for the fragmented
character that it now assumes.

The year 1895, as I have recorded elsewhere, was an
exceptionally busy one for Mr Sherlock Holmes and was
the herald, indeed, of that period of unceasing, intense
activity that lasted until his retirement from professional
consultancy work some eight years later. My small
Kensington practice having been purchased by young
Verner (with Holmes's assistance, as I subsequently discovered), I was free to accompany my friend on a good many of
his expeditions and to assist him wherever I could, although
I can scarcely flatter myself that my ruminations and
suggestions contributed anything of great substance to the
eventual outcome of his investigations. But my obser-
vations, such as they were, almost invariably received his
full attention and were sometimes the unwitting means

of setting him off in a totally opposite (and, it would transpire, far more rewarding) direction. He would also use me as a sounding board for various theories of his own when they were still at the semi-formulated stage, being convinced that a second opinion, on such occasions, was always of some value. At other times, however, when engaged on cases of either a particularly abtruse or a confidential nature, he would make no attempt to enlist my services and I knew better than to press them where they were not required.

His powers were now at their height. Throughout this hectic year, in which scarcely a week went by without some new and deeply mystifying problem being brought to his attention by a range of clients which varied from the highest to the lowest in the land, I was aware that he still pondered upon the Drood affair and that he made, from time to time, some further attempts to probe it. Correspondence with the local Kent constabulary and approaches to the Criminal Investigation Department of Scotland Yard resulted in confirmation that the official file on Edwin Drood, insofar as it had ever existed, had long ago been closed and enquiries in the vicinity of Staples Inn brought to light no news of Neville Landless. It was established that Hiram Grewgious, the one-time guardian of Miss Rosa Bud, had also resided at Staples Inn but had died some twelve years before. 'You will doubtless be familiar, Watson,' he said on one occasion, 'with a certain pursuit, popular on race tracks and at street corners alike, of "Find the Lady". Well, I am trying to find *two* ladies – one of them still moderately young and the other (if she is still with us) extremely old.' I was aware of the "Baker Street irregulars" being called in to assist with one or both of these searches, but I was not aware of any successful outcome.

'Holmes,' I once asked, 'why do you go on with these enquiries?'

'Curiosity, my dear chap; sheer, simple curiosity. Some strange things happened in Cloisterham twenty-five years ago and for my own peace of mind, if nothing else, I would dearly love to get to the bottom of them.'

Then towards the conclusion of breakfast, one morning late in February, he pushed back his coffee cup and remarked, with a twinkle in his eye, 'What say you, Watson, to a further meeting with Mr John Jasper?'

'You've tracked him down, then?' I exclaimed in astonishment.

'Tush, man, that was no great problem. Having established that he was suffering from amnesia, and that he was clearly not a free agent but under restraint of some kind, with two solicitous gentlemen ever concerned about his whereabouts on those occasions (at least two) when he managed to evade that restraint, all that remained to be done was to locate the institution in which he was housed. You will recall that his letter was posted in Surrey – from Guildford, to be precise – and a scrutiny of the excellent Ordance Survey map for that area showed that there were three such establishments in that part of the world. Telegrams to the two nearest at hand produced negative results, but I have struck gold with the third.' And he passed me a telegram which ran, 'Your surmise correct. John Jasper has been resident in this asylum since 1871. James

93

Wakefield, Warden, Stazeby Nanton.'

'And our seeing him again will serve some useful purpose?'

'Ah, that I can't say! But it is worth a visit, I think, and even if Mr Jasper himself is uncommunicative the warden may be able to shed some light upon his curious state of mind. Technically, of course, he remains my client, although the prospect of my ever receiving a fee for my services now seems decidedly remote.'

And so it was that three hours later a pony and trap from the nearest railway station, some four miles distant from the establishment itself, carried us through bleak, unappealing, midwinter countryside to the asylum of Stazeby Nanton. The building itself was an impressive mansion, set in extensive grounds which were surrounded by a high red-brick wall. A formidable porter, in the lodge at the main gates, scrutinized us closely before sanctioning our entrance and I noticed, as we came nearer the house, that some of the windows were barred.

Mr James Wakefield, a dark-haired, short, fussy and rather self-important little man, his stub of a nose surmounted by a large pair of horn-rimmed spectacles, greeted us in the entrance hall (in the presence of two or three members of staff as burly as the lodge-keeper, all of whom surveyed us just as keenly) and bustled us into his well-furnished study. 'Pray be seated, gentlemen,' he began. 'I am, of course, familiar with your reputation, Mr Holmes. What can I do for you?'

'I am interested', replied Holmes, 'in whatever you can tell me about the history and state of mind of Mr John

Jasper. Perhaps you have a file of papers on this gentleman? You stated in your telegram, I believe, that he had been an inmate of this establishment since 1871.'

'Not an inmate, gentlemen, but a *resident*,' returned Mr Wakefield primly. 'A file is not necessary for our present purposes, for I have been here almost as long as Mr Jasper himself. I arrived at Stazeby Nanton twenty-four years ago next August, by which time he had been in residence for six months, and am fully acquainted with every detail of his case – or, at least, with every detail that can be humanly ascertained. I have known this worthy gentleman so long and so intimately that I might almost claim, in the fullest possible sense, to be my brother's keeper.'

'And he is no doubt a peerless kinsman,' said Holmes drily. 'Yet I believe – forgive me, for no slight is intended – that there have been one or two occasions when Mr Jasper has not been kept as well as he might have been?'

'Mr Holmes!' exclaimed the warden in outrage. 'You must understand, once and for all, that Stazeby Nanton is *not* a prison. It is operated on the most enlightened and philanthropic of principles for the benefit of those members of the more genteel or select of our classes who, for one reason or another, find themselves either temporarily or permanently unable to cope with the stresses and strains of modern life or who are subject to unfortunate delusions or confusions. Stazeby Nanton was established some forty years ago and has acquired a status of some repute with the passing of those years. You may be interested to learn that its activities received the personal blessing of Mr Luke Honeythunder (whose statue you doubtless observed in the village on your arrival) and that it was, indeed, the Honeythunder Bequest which has enabled it to thrive, and build upon that reputation, during the past decade or so. The twenty residents are not always, perhaps, so free to come and go as you or I might be, and it might sometimes happen that a departure of an unauthorized nature is effected, but they are not criminals, Mr Holmes, and no attempt is made to treat them as such. They move freely within the limits of the house (unless confined to their quarters for medical reasons) and meet one another, if they so desire, at the dinner-table and in a residents' lounge. Or they can, of course, remain in their rooms if the fancy so takes them.'

'I stand corrected,' said my companion, deferentially. 'Nevertheless, you will be aware that Mr Jasper called upon me two months ago, to all intents and purposes master of his own destiny, and presented me with an intriguing problem to ponder upon. You will appreciate my surprise at discovering that he was apparently under some form of restraint – although my mind is greatly relieved at learning that he is in such good hands as your own – and Dr Watson and I, having made this gentleman's acquaintance, would be interested in learning more of his ailment. It may have some bearing upon whether or not we should continue with our investigations.'

Mr Wakefield, mollified to some extent, recollected his duties as host and poured a glass of port for each of us. 'Mr Jasper', he said, resuming his seat behind his splendid desk, 'suffers from two delusions of a singular nature. He is convinced that he is living in the year 1870 and he is also convinced, for much of the time, that he is living in his small apartment in the town of Cloisterham. All evidence and information to the contrary fails to impinge upon his consciousness and we have reached the point, I must confess, when we no longer endeavour to make him think otherwise. The only item of information that he has assimilated in recent years, Mr Holmes, has been the fact of your own existence, and he has followed the news of your exploits with remarkable intentness. You are now incorporated, as it were, in his 1870 scenario. The news of your apparent death plunged him into gloom, but the recent revelation that you were alive after all and had returned to Baker Street was greeted with intense excitement and apparently determined his resolve to write to you and seek your assistance.'

'I am most flattered! But can you explain how the letter came to bear the correct 1894 date and how, indeed, it came to be sent to me at all?'

'One of the other residents, with whom he has struck up an acquaintance,' said Mr Wakefield, rather grimly, 'thoughtfully inserted the date on his behalf and also arranged for the letter to be dispatched, on Mr Jasper's behalf, by a relation who visited him on that day. Needless to say, Mr Holmes, the staff of this establishment were totally unaware that such a communication had been dispatched (for all outgoing post is, as a rule, scrutinized most vigorously) and I have taken the necessary steps to ensure that such a breach of procedure does not occur again.'

'And Mr Jasper's visit to me was itself, of course, a breach of procedure – an "unauthorized departure", as you phrased it earlier?'

'Yes, most certainly! Fortunately, we were able to ascertain from the other person – from the other resident – his most likely destination, and my staff were able to apprehend him the moment he left your premises.'

'An operation most skilfully executed,' said Holmes, with a gentle touch of sarcasm. 'And can you furnish me, Mr Wakefield, with rather more precise details of the form that Mr Jasper's malady takes?'

'For the greater part of the time,' said the warden, absent-mindedly fondling his gold watch and chain, 'he seems as sane as you or I and it is possible to converse with him on a wide range of subjects. He is a cultivated man and not without a sense of humour. But there are occasions when he works himself up into the most ferocious rages, seemingly possessed by a demoniacal fury, and has to be physically restrained before he can do the other residents or, indeed, himself some dreadful injury. At other times again, he sinks into a mood of bewildered apathy in which he recognizes nobody and seems oblivious of his surroundings.'

'But these outbreaks,' I said, 'distressing though they must be, are presumably not uncommon among your residents and not confined to Mr Jasper alone?'

'No, Dr Watson, such moods are all too familiar to those of us who labour in the vineyard at Stazeby Nanton. What is quite unique, however, is Mr Jasper's fixation about the year 1870. His behaviour in this respect follows what is basically an unchanging pattern. He was originally much distressed, as you are no doubt aware, by the disappearance of his nephew on the Christmas Eve of 1869. At the beginning of the year he is in a state of great perturbation. By the end of February (the present time, in fact) he has become more resigned to his loss but is bent upon bringing the villain of the piece, a Mr Landless, to justice. In the months of June and July he grows greatly agitated and it is usually at that time that we experience the violence which I referred to just now. By the late autumn he becomes more relaxed, as though things are going well, and is almost invariably amiable. At the approach of Christmas, however, he becomes steadily more excited. By the time Christmas Day itself dawns he has taken utter leave of his senses, being appallingly confused and suffering, obviously, from the after-effects of some terrible shock of which he cannot bear to retain the remembrance. He remains in this state for several weeks. The cycle then resumes. Every year he grows older, and the century draws towards its end, but every year he is totally convinced that he is living again through that traumatic year of 1870. At times he is, admittedly, quite capable of realizing that he is *not* living in Cloisterham, but those times are few and far between — and I am not certain that such realizations, when they come, are necessarily all to the good.'

'Thank you, Mr Wakefield,' said Holmes. 'A most graphic account. And does he have many visitors?'

'No, none at all. Although it is not generally known, I believe, that he resides here, for the Cathedral authorities were very unwilling that the news of his breakdown should become public knowledge. He apparently had no surviving relations and no close friends.'

'And who pays for his board and lodging?'

'The Public Trustee, in co-operation with the Cathedral authorities. Mr Jasper is a relatively wealthy man and there is no danger of his not being well provided for. His apartment in Cloisterham, I understand, remains just as it was twenty-five years ago, in the theoretical expectation of his eventual return, but I fear that will never be.'

'And how does he occupy himself?'

'By writing, reading and singing. And also in prayer – for he is, of course, most religious – although he usually seems to have some strange difficulty in effectively terminating his devotions, and they appear to degenerate into incoherent mumblings. He is hardly ever a relaxed man, Mr Holmes, and I'm tempted to say that he has never enjoyed a proper night's sleep since he's been here. It is, at times, necessary to sedate him.'

'And would I be correct in surmising that it was also in the month of December that he made an earlier escape – I beg your pardon, an "unauthorized departure" – some twelve years ago?'

Mr Wakefield looked surprised but nodded. 'Yes, that's right, Mr Holmes.'

'And that he was apprehended in East London in rather curious circumstances?'

'Good heavens!' exclaimed Mr Wakefield, in genuine astonishment. 'However did you know that? Yes, as I have said, he always becomes especially restless as the festive season approaches. It is clear that we shall have to keep an even closer eye on him in the future.'

But your security measures are most impressive. I am

surprised that he has managed to elude the vigilance of your staff on two occasions.'

Mr Wakefield shrugged his shoulders. 'Where there's a will, Mr Holmes,' he remarked, 'the way will invariably present itself.'

'Very true. And as he has managed the seemingly impossible on two occasions, there seems every likelihood, however elaborate the precautions you adopt, that he will repeat his success. I wonder, Mr Wakefield, in the event of a *third* "unauthorized departure", whether you could notify me of the event without delay?'

Mr Wakefield, still impressed by my colleague's reference to the East London incident (which had equally impressed myself), willingly promised to do so.

'And now, if you have no objection, perhaps we could pay our respects to Mr Jasper? I assure you we shall not trouble him for long.'

Mr Wakefield had no objection of any kind and shepherded us up to a room on the first floor, pausing a while until he had selected the appropriate key from the bundle which had been hanging in his study. The large room into which he showed us did bear, curiously, a quite striking resemblance to the rooms over the gatehouse except that there was no piano. There were shelves with a number of books on them, two small barred windows not unlike their latticed counterparts and two comfortable chairs by a fireplace, in one of which sat the choir-master of Cloisterham.

I was shocked by the change in his appearance. He had looked haggard on the previous occasion: he looked doubly so now. His hair had then been heavily streaked with grey: it was now all but white. A pair of deeply sunken eyes gazed uncomprehendingly at us and he endeavoured, with a shaking hand, to rise from his seat. He failed and fell back again, collapsing into it like an elderly marionette.

'Please don't disturb yourself, Mr Jasper,' said Holmes softly. 'You may remember that I am Sherlock Holmes and that you came to see me a little while ago.'

'Sherlock Holmes,' the old man repeated to himself. 'Sherlock Holmes,' he said again, and this time there was the faint glimmer of a dawning recollection.

Holmes lowered himself into the other chair and Mr Wakefield and I remained standing at the door.

'Sherlock Holmes,' said Mr Jasper for a third time, and this time with an air of triumph. 'Why, I thought I'd dreamt you!' And he gazed at my colleague with a mixture of elation and wonderment.

'You came to see me,' said Holmes. 'About your nephew.'

'Yes, yes!' exclaimed the old man, in excited confirmation. 'And I thought, afterwards, that it must all have been a dream — though how I could dream about you since I never sleep (or do I?), is more than I can say!'

'I called in', continued Holmes gently, 'to reassure you, Mr Jasper, that enquiries are proceeding. I hope to have some news for you one of these days.'

Mr Jasper waited hungrily for more, his eyes narrowing as he scrutinized my friend's face. But Holmes remained silent. 'And have you', asked Mr Jasper at length, 'apprehended Neville Landless for that foul deed?'

'Not yet, Mr Jasper,' returned Holmes. 'But be patient.'

'I rely solely on you, Mr Holmes — and my dear boy relies upon you, for I know he is near me — to bring that villain to justice. Incapacitated as I am at present (for my good friend yonder tells me I must stay in the gatehouse until restored to health), I am dependent upon you, Mr Holmes, to act as my eyes and ears. Rot his hide!' And with this extraordinary cry he jerked himself to his feet, virtually clawing at the air, before toppling back again and glaring at us all with terrible eyes from the depth of his chair.

We left Stazeby Nanton soon afterwards. It had not been a pleasant visit and for some time neither Holmes nor I spoke. The pony and trap bore us back to the station and we caught the train to London a little while later. By degrees, normality returned.

'I seriously wonder, Holmes,' I said at length, 'whether there is anything to be gained from pursuing these enquiries. Is it not simply morbid curiosity that drives you on? Mr Jasper, semi-demented as we saw him just now, is scarcely your usual type of client and we really seem to have come to a full stop. The Crisparkles know something but will obviously not assist us and the other characters in this drama, if they are not actually deceased, have vanished into thin air. After 1870 we have no idea what happened to them.'

'Not quite,' came the response. 'I am able to inform you, for example, that Miss Bud married a Mr Jack Tartar, a retired officer of the Royal Navy, in April 1872 and that she gave birth to a daughter, Florence, in the spring of 1874. They were living, at that time, in a cottage in Hampstead, but subsequently moved on.'

'By all that's marvellous, Holmes!' I exclaimed. 'However did you find this out?'

My companion shrugged his shoulders. 'Elementary in the extreme,' he responded, with a slight touch of impatience. 'We were aware that Miss Rosa had become engaged towards the end of 1870 – or so, at least, Mr Jasper was given to understand – and an hour or two's research in the records of Somerset House sufficed to yield the relevant facts. A remarkable repository of information, Watson, and a source unaccountably neglected by the English detective force! The annals of that building, setting out births, marriages and deaths over the past sixty years, complete with details of addresses, occupations and ages, present us with an unparalleled number of peepholes into the past. The place is a veritable time machine. But it is the present we are concerned with, and I must confess that the current location of the Tartar family is totally unknown to me. The Admiralty records of officers on the retired list are, I regret to say, woefully incomplete. It may be that some enquiries initiated in the Portsmouth area will prove more felicitous, but I have my doubts.'

'And is there anything else that you discovered at Somerset House, Holmes?'

'There is one line of enquiry that I have, certainly, neglected to pursue and I must follow that one up as soon as opportunity permits. But time is in short supply, my dear fellow, and it is the harassment of Mr John Vincent Harden which requires my more immediate attention.'

11

Bringing the persecutors of the tobacco millionaire to book, however, was a task that overlapped with our involvement in the tale of Miss Violet Smith, chronicled elsewhere as 'The Solitary Cyclist', and no sooner had *that* been brought to a satisfactory conclusion than the strange business at the Priory school was upon us. Then came three weeks in one of our great University towns, where Holmes (in the midst of carrying out some crucial research into Early English charters) was caught up in the intriguing problem of the Fortescue Scholarship. This was succeeded by the singular episode of the six Napoleons. The next item on the agenda was the mysterious death of Cardinal Tosca, which Holmes investigated at the specific request of His Holiness the Pope. This was followed by a variety of other commissions. No sooner had Wilson, the infamous canary-breeder of East London, been placed under lock and key than we were involved in the Woodman Lea affair and the hideous murder of Captain Peter Carey. In the second week of July I accompanied Holmes to Norway, in an investigation into the circumstances surrounding the mysterious death of

Halvard Solness (the precise details of which, I regret to say, I am still not at liberty to divulge). At the end of that month Holmes was summoned to the Vatican, to clarify some outstanding matters relating to the Tosca affair, where he was granted a personal audience with His Holiness. On the return journey he stopped off in Paris, to be presented by the French President with the Order of the Legion of Honour for the instrumental role he had played in helping to track down Huret, the Boulevard assassin.

I was left to my own devices for some two weeks, therefore, and found the period of unaccustomed repose by no means unwelcome. I devoted some of the time to pure relaxation and the rest of it to putting my papers in order and writing up the case notes of some of Holmes's earlier investigations. It was while I was thus preoccupied, one sunny day in early August, that Thurston dropped in and insisted on bearing me away from what he regarded as my tedious labours. I accompanied him, albeit with somewhat muted enthusiasm, to the summer exhibition at the Royal Academy, which had attracted its usual clientele to gaze at what were, by and large, the usual somewhat insipid offerings. There was, however, one picture which was attracting a fair degree of attention from the passing throng.

'By Jove, old lad!' murmured Thurston, as we drew near. 'She's a bit of a stunner, eh?'

The painting in question, entitled 'Morning Glory', depicted a young girl wearing a pale blue dress sitting in a garden under a parasol on what was obviously a glorious summer's day, an impish expression on her face and long brown hair cascading down her back. She was undoubtedly, as Thurston had put it, a 'bit of a stunner', and I grunted my assent.

'Ah,' said Thurston, consulting his catalogue. 'One of Dupont's latest productions – I might have guessed. Basically one of the Impressionist school, and owing a lot to that chap Renoir, but he seems to spend more time in this country than he does in France. One of our home-grown Impressionists, you might say.'

The name was familiar to me, since Edmund Dupont was as well known as an illustrator of books (especially children's fairy tales) as he was as a portrait painter. What was vaguely disturbing, however, was the fact that the portrait also seemed familiar. I could not call to mind having met the young lady in question but was convinced that I had nevertheless somehow encountered her, and in the not too distant past. It was not until later that night, as I tossed and turned in the early hours, trying in vain to lose myself in slumber, that the answer came. The portrait had something in common with the amateurish daub of Rosa Bud that Holmes and I had seen in Mr Jasper's gatehouse living-room.

The following day I returned to Burlington House and gazed for some time at the portrait. The features, so far as I could recall those of the earlier picture, were by no means precisely the same, but when every allowance had been made for the difference in styles and skills the two portraits did indeed have much in common – including the fact, I was now startled to find (although I may have marked it subconsciously the previous day), that the dresses of *both* sitters were adorned with a brooch composed of an amethyst in an extremely intricate gold setting that resembled a budding rose.

The coincidence, I concluded at last, was too great to be ignored. It might well be that there was more than one such brooch, but the similarity between the faces of the wearers was unmistakable. I had assumed, it being five months since our second meeting with Mr Jasper, and taking into account the number of cases with which Holmes had become involved since then, that he had abandoned his investigations into the Drood affair, and − for reasons indicated already − I had been rather relieved at this. But I was aware that he had been trying hard, at one time, to ascertain the whereabouts of Mrs Jack Tartar, the former Miss Rosa Bud, and I was excited by the possibility that I might succeed where Holmes had failed.

My mind made up, I had a word with the attendant in that particular room and was directed to the staff of the Academy offices for further information. I was immensely interested, I told them, in the painting entitled 'Morning Glory' and wondered if they could supply me with further details of both the artist and his address. This they obligingly did, indicating (in the process) that there was no great secret about any of the information. M. Dupont, it transpired, was indeed of French extraction, but had escaped from Paris at the time when it was under siege in the Franco-Prussian war, had made his way to London in company with many of his compatriots, and (unlike most of those compatriots) had remained in England when the war came to an end. He had established an impressive reputation, both as a portrait painter and as a book illustrator, and his services were much in demand by a number of publishers, both in England and on the Continent. He was now, it seemed, living in Peckham, and they supplied me with the address in case I wished to write to him.

Throwing caution to the winds, however, I resolved to get in touch with M. Dupont without delay. Hastening to Charing Cross I caught the first available train to the leafy suburbs of Peckham and, within two hours of leaving the Academy, turned in at the gate of a large house in Linden Grove. Before I could pull the bellrope at the front door, however, it burst open and a short, dapper gentleman with pince-nez and pointed beard burst out in some excitement, carrying a travelling bag and umbrella, evidently with an urgent appointment to keep. He was dressed in a smart brown suit of check design and wearing a bowler hat, quite unlike the garb which I associated with artists (although my first-hand experience of them was, admittedly, somewhat limited). He pulled up short at the sight of me and, despite his hurry, came to a halt, raised his hat and bowed stiffly from the waist. I returned his salutation and introduced myself, noting as I did so that M. Dupont had a slightly blotchy face and surmising that his poor skin complexion might account for the beard.

'*Bonjour, monsieur!*' he exclaimed. 'And to what do I owe ze pleasure of zees visit?'

'I have just come from the Royal Academy,' I explained, 'where you have a painting of a young girl, 'Morning Glory', on display.'

'*Mais, oui!* You like it, yes?'

'I like it enormously,' I confessed. 'But the fact is, M. Dupont —'

'Ah, no!' he exclaimed. 'Ze painting, she is not for sale. *Non, monsieur*, in zees I cannot oblige you.'

'No,' I said, 'that's not the point. The thing is —'

But again, he would not allow me to finish. *'Non, non!'* he exclaimed impatiently, with much waving of the arms. 'Ze picture is not on ze market, I cannot part wiz it, not for — 'ow you say? — not for ze King's ransom.'

'But I don't want to buy it!' I almost shrieked, aware of how absurd this scene was as we both stood there on the garden path.

M. Dupont stopped gesticulating and gazed at me in astonishment. 'You don't want to buy it?' he repeated, in evident disbelief. 'You don't want to buy my painting?' His face grew thunderous as the sheer enormity of what I had said evidently sank in.

'It is a marvellous painting,' I hastened to reassure him, 'but the fact is I believe I know — that is, I am distantly acquainted with — the young lady in question. I am very anxious to see her and wonder whether you could possibly let me know where she is living.'

'Zounds!' exclaimed the artist. 'Zis is a new ploy, You Zinc I introduce you to my sitter, yes? You zinc I bring togezzer ze elderly military gentleman and ze pretty young girl, yes? *Mon Dieu*, ze Eenglish have ze cheek of ze very Devil!'

'Sir,' I cried,' you are grossly insulting. My intentions are, I assure you, strictly honourable.'

He grew extremely red in the face and I fear that I did the

same. I somehow managed to convince him, in the end, that I had no underhand motives in making this request, that I believed the young lady in question was a Mrs Jack Tartar, formerly a Miss Rosa Bud, and that I was very anxious to establish contact with her with a view to exchanging some information to our mutual benefit. M. Dupont listened impassively to these remarks, neither denying nor confirming the identity of his sitter. 'Zees iz ze strange kettle of ze fish,' he concluded at length. '*Monsieur*, I have ze train to catch – I have ze urgent appointment in Hampshire. I must refer you to my clerk, yes? You give eem ze full particulars and we consider further on zees matter.'

He bowed stiffly, stepped back into the house for a moment and summoned his secretary to attend to me. 'And now,' he announced, 'I must run, as you English say, like ze clappers, no? *Monsieur*, good day!'

And with that he disappeared down the drive, his legs twinkling rapidly and his umbrella and travelling bag swinging wildly. I gazed after him, concluding that, for someone who had spent so many years in England, he had a remarkably poor command of the language.

I was relieved to find that his clerk, at any rate, was English. The gentleman noted down, albeit in a disbelieving fashion, the details of my request, snorting and puffing as he did so. 'We shall be . . .' he said, and paused.

'Yes?' I asked at length.

'In contact,' said he, and closed the door.

I was disconcerted by these exchanges and resolved to say nothing about them to Holmes, when he returned, until such time as they had achieved (if it were possible) some

111

tangible result. I could not help reflecting, as I walked glumly away through the sun-dappled streets of Nunhead, that my colleague would have handled things somewhat differently.

12

'Come, Watson!' exclaimed Holmes's impatient voice, which was accompanied by a vigorous shaking of my shoulder. 'There is a cab waiting at the door and no time to lose. We must be up and away! And bring your bag,' he added. 'I have need of your professional services.'

I was thus rudely awoken, one dark, chilly morning in mid-October, by my friend in one of his most brusque, intolerant of moods, but I wasted no time in recriminations. I pulled on my clothes, noting that Holmes himself, as he paced up and down the room, was wearing a remarkably long overcoat and carrying a small carpet bag, and within five minutes we were clattering away through the slow-clearing mists of autumn, which had succeeded in penetrating even into Baker Street. We were heading, I noted after a time, in an easterly direction and the cab threaded its way through the heavy morning traffic of the City, past the Honeythunder Memorial, into the streets of Stepney and thence towards the docks.

Holmes, tensed up all this time, like a greyhound straining at the leash, barely uttered a sound until we were on the last lap of our journey, when it suddenly occurred to him tha: something in the way of an apology (and also an explanation) was due. 'I am sorry for the rush, my dear chap,' he began, 'but it was less than an hour ago that young Dawkins arrived hotfoot with the news and we cannot afford to waste a single moment. The irregulars have finally tracked down one of my missing ladies, but she is on her last legs and I fear that, if this confounded traffic jam does not clear in the near future, we may yet be too late.'

He gazed moodily out of the window, drumming his fingers against the clasp of the bag, then permitted himself a brief smile. 'I have, I fear, been withholding certain particulars from you for far too long, Watson,' he continued, 'and you have borne the suspense with commendable patience.' (Aware, as I was, that I for my part had not been altogether frank with Holmes, for I had received a curt note from M. Dupont a day or two before to the effect that the young lady depicted in his painting had no knowledge of a Dr Watson and that there must therefore be some mistake, I guiltily waved aside this remark with the most subdued of deprecatory rejoinders.)

'You will be aware', went on my friend, 'that from time to time, and particularly in the earlier part of my career, it has sometimes been necessary for me to frequent the opium dens of East London in search of information. Some twelve or thirteen years ago I chanced to be imbibing (in the guise of a Lascar seaman) the delights of a particularly insalubrious establishment presided over by an old woman known, to all her clients, as "the Princess Puffa". I say "old" because she undoubtedly seemed greatly advanced in years, although you will be familiar, of course, with the fact that opium has a peculiar ageing effect upon those of its addicts who sample it upon anything approaching a regular basis. It may be that she was no more than in her mid-sixties when I saw her last, but she had long borne the reputation of being a secret midnight hag *par excellence* – in certain underworld circles, indeed, something of a celebrity! At one time, I believe, small groups of distinguished visitors were escorted to her premises by senior members of the local constabulary, and she was in some danger of becoming what might almost be termed "a tourist attraction". Some eight years ago, however, Princess Puffa retired from her trade, and until young Dawkins (who is now guiding our driver) arrived this morning I had no means of knowing whether she was alive or dead.'

Holmes gazed, reminiscently, through the window. 'On the occasion of which I speak,' he continued, 'the only other patrons of the Puffa establishment were two Chinamen, both of them in a state of insensibility. I was making up my mind to leave, for my particular quest on that occasion was evidently proving fruitless, when a well-dressed gentleman, with a rather wild expression on his face, suddenly joined the clientele. That gentleman was John Jasper.'

I reacted with astonishment to this news and Holmes smiled. 'Your own surprise', said he, 'was fully equalled, if not surpassed, by that of the Princess Puffa, who appeared to be dumbfounded in amazement – and, what was still more interesting, gave every appearance of being terrified out of her wits. "So you've come again, deary," she croaked out at length. "It's been a long time. The mixture as before, was it? Sit yourself down, and I'll mix it for ye." This she proceeded to do, with trembling hand, and Mr Jasper gazed intently about him in the mean time. I feigned unconsciousness but contrived to observe, through half-closed eyes, what followed. He took the mixture, complaining that it was not so potent as it had been previously, but within half an hour he had fallen into a deep slumber in which he twitched and groaned to himself. The old woman, after reassuring herself that the rest of us were still asleep, plucked up her courage and approached the recumbent body of our friend. "Oh, you're a fine one, you are!" she cried, shaking her fist at him, and then – so incensed did she become – she actually kicked him, twice or thrice, so that he groaned and cried out, while not awakening. Her feelings thus relieved, she hastened away – to return, some little time later, with a police constable in tow! She pointed at our friend and there was a certain amount of whispering which I was unable to catch. "Not in here, you don't!" she hissed at one point. "Suppose he comes back here again? No, it's outside for you, my lad!" and she bundled the constable out of her den. Some forty minutes then elapsed, in which she resumed her place in her chair while watching Mr Jasper intently all the time.

'Our friend eventually regained his senses and staggered to his feet, declining her casual offer of another dose and complaining yet again, this time to the effect that the "vision" had been so poor as to scarcely justify his coming. Before leaving her den, however, he scrutinized both my two companions, listening intently to such mutterings as they gave rise to. When he came to myself I obligingly uttered some gibberish which he decided, at length, signified nothing. "Unintelligible!" he exclaimed, threw down some coins for the Princess (which she spat upon, the moment his back was turned, and swept contemptuously to the floor) and took his leave. I promptly regained my own consciousness, perhaps rather *too* promptly, for she gave me a mighty suspicious look, settled up my account and then hastened in his footsteps. I found that he had been detained, a short distance from the Puffa establishment, by the constable I had seen previously and by another one as well. But the affair was, of course, none of my business and my curiosity had to remain unassuaged. You can imagine my astonishment when, twelve years later, this particular client appeared in Baker Street! That was my first encounter with John Jasper and my last with Princess Puffa — but one of the tales of Mr Datchery told by our friend the Dean, which you will doubtless recall, strongly suggests that she had made her way to Cloisterham on at least one occasion and it is vital that we find out what she knows. The fact that she is alive at all is nothing short of a miracle, but her time has come and she is, so I gather, not long for this world.'

The cab eventually halted at one of the most dismal of the dockland hovels and Holmes, preceded by young Dawkins (playing Gooseberry, as it were), hastened inside. 'She's a-going fast, sir,' I heard a voice say, 'you're only just in time.' I paid the driver, instructing him to return in an hour, and followed Holmes into a darkened room from which the most revolting of stenches was emanating. On a tiny bed in the corner lay a very old woman. Another woman, who had been in attendance, bobbed as we came in

117

and made herself scarce, hovering in the vicinity of the door and shaking her head sorrowfully. Dawkins retreated into the background and Holmes bent over the poor creature on the bed.

'So here we are again, Princess Puffa!' he said, quietly and almost jovially.

The old woman opened her eyes and slowly brought Holmes into focus. 'I dunno you,' she muttered.

'Ah, but you do, you know! But I looked rather different on the last occasion that we met.'

Princess Puffa continued to gaze at him uncomprehendingly. She was, all too clearly, on the last lap of her journey and in no mood to bandy words with strangers.

'Look to the lady, Watson,' murmured Holmes, straightening up, and he disappeared into the darkness of the room behind me. I did what I could for the poor woman, which was little enough in the circumstances, and she contrived to nod her head in gratitude and mutter, 'Thank ye! Thank ye!'

Some minutes went by, and then . . .

'Do you know me now?' asked Holmes gently, reappearing at the bedside. He had donned the Datchery wig (freshly laundered since its last appearance), together with the Datchery hat, and was clad in a blue surtout. I am not at all certain that I would have recognized him had we passed in the street.

The old woman's face positively lit up and she struggled to raise herself on her elbow. 'It's the dear old gentleman!' she exclaimed in joy. 'Yes, of course I know you now, dearie. Fancy it being you all the time!'

'You remember we met in Cloisterham?'

She nodded, with great vigour.

'And do you remember Mr John Jasper?'

'Remember him?' she screeched, with terrible vehemence. 'Oh, yes, I remember *him* all right, don't *you* worry! I'd remember him for a thousand years, and then some.'

'And you remember what you told me about him?'

Again, a vigorous nod, followed by much coughing.

'Could you tell me again, do you think?'

'But I told you it all once, dearie,' she pleaded, looking perplexed. 'You knows it all.'

'But my friend here', said Datchery-Holmes, indicating myself, 'was not present then and he would dearly love to hear it from your own lips. Come, one last favour.'

'John Jasper was the organist,' she said, 'in the Kin-free-der-ell.'

'That's it! And he came to see you in London, didn't he?'

'That he did!' was jerked out of the poor woman, with nods galore. 'Many and many a time. Oh yes, *didn't* he come and see me, though!'

'And what happened?'

'He sang so sweetly – or leastways, he did in the early days – and he had this dream, about someone called Ned, and about what he was going to do to him. Over and over again, he had it!'

'And then?'

'And then I tried to track him back to his lair, for the third time, and that was when you saw me and that was when I told you everything I knew.'

'But what about those other occasions? Your first and second visits to the town?'

'That first time, as I told you, he gave me the slip and I didn't even get as far as the town. That second time, on the Christmas Eve, I didn't do much better, neither, except at the very end of the day I met that nice young man called Edwin who gave me three-and-six for me lodgings and me fare back to London.'

'Did you, indeed?' exclaimed Holmes involuntarily, and slightly out of his assumed character. But Princess Puffa, engulfed in a fit of coughing, failed to notice. 'But what of Ned?'

'No,' she said sadly, after clearing her throat, 'I couldn't find no Ned.'

'And you had wanted to warn him?'

'Oh yes,' she exclaimed, emphatically nodding her head, 'I wanted to tell him, see. But the next time that Jasper came, just before I met you, I knew it was too late. He'd done for Ned, though he seemed none the happier for it — and the dream warn't the same, neither!'

'How so?'

"'Cos he saw somethink that he hadn't seen before, dearie, and he didn't like it one little bit, not he!'

'And did you ever see Mr Jasper again?'

'Once more, dearie, and that was many years arter — but I settled his hash *then*, all right! I soon got him back where he belonged, didn't I just!'

'You knew where he belonged, then?'

'I'd kept tabs on him, all right. It was that —' and she used an expression which indicated that she was fully acquainted with Stazeby Nanton and the purpose it served. The vehemence with which she ejaculated that expression brought on another fit of coughing, and I knew that the end was near.

'There is just one thing more, Princess,' said Holmes, with a rather curious expression on his face. 'Did you have any ulterior purpose of your own in keeping tabs on Mr Jasper? Was it simply the desire to have justice meted out in respect of this unknown Ned, or did you have a private score to settle? Had Mr Jasper done you or your family wrong at some distant period in the past?'

The old woman, looking greatly excited, again tried to rouse herself but the effort was too much. She fell back but continued muttering. My friend bent low, listening intently, but the sound gradually faded away.

'Unintelligible,' said Holmes at last, straightening up. And he slowly removed his hat and wig.

13

It seemed, in a sense, that the mystery of Edwin Drood had finally been solved. All the information at our disposal pointed to the fact, horrible though it was, that John Jasper had been responsible for the murder of his own nephew and for the disappearance of the body. Yet this conclusion was curiously unsatisfactory and I knew that Holmes himself remained far from happy about the point at which our investigation had apparently terminated. 'There is', he said on one occasion, as the winter evenings drew on and we pulled our chairs closer to the fire, 'something not right here. If Mr Jasper was the murderer, why should he be so obsessed in bringing the alleged villain of the piece to justice? He himself was, after all, clearly above suspicion. Had it not been for the vehemence with which, in his semi-demented state, he has pursued Neville Landless, we ourselves would not have been drawn into the affair and the revelations of Princess Puffa would have remained a closed book for evermore. One can only surmise that Mr Jaspher wanted it to be clearly established that somebody else was definitely responsible for the crime. "To be thus is nothing, but to be *safely* thus" is a dictum which murderers have certainly been known to practise, yet in this instance I am not at all sure that it fits the bill. The story remains tantalizingly incomplete and we know, as yet, less than half the facts.'

So matters stood until, three days before Christmas, I chanced to linger at the breakfast table over the columns of *The Times* rather longer than my normal wont (a result of having been tempted into an additional cup of Mrs Hudson's coffee). Casting a brief eye over the announcements of births, deaths and marriages, while my companion skimmed rapidly through his post, I happened to glimpse a not unfamiliar name in the adjoining column and let out a cry which attracted his attention.

'Good gracious, Holmes!' I exclaimed. 'Listen to this, from the "In Memoriam" column — "Landless. In everloving memory of Neville Landless, a dear brother and friend. 'Love is Immortal and Life is Eternal.' Helena and Septimus."'

Holmes snatched the paper out of my hands and read the entry over to himself. His expression, much to my surprise, was one of intense annoyance — but of annoyance at himself, I soon realized, rather than anyone else. 'I have been slow, Watson,' he exclaimed, 'damnably slow! I half suspected this months ago but there was always some other matter of particular urgency on hand ... Procrastination, my dear fellow, is ever the culprit! Pray Heavens that I am not too late to make amends.'

He left the house almost instantly and several hours elapsed before he returned, exhausted but seemingly triumphant. 'I have done all I can,' he said, 'and we must await the outcome.' He poked the fire vigorously and flung himself into his favourite armchair. I judged the moment propitious for making a small confession.

'Holmes,' said I, 'there is something which I ought to have mentioned to you before now, except that it is information of a purely negative kind. Whether it has any relevance at all to your investigations must be for you to decide.' I then told him about that visit to the Royal Academy with Thurston, the coincidence of the apparent similarity between the two portraits (seemingly supported by the rosebud brooch), of my subsequent farcical encounter with M. Dupont and, finally, of the curt note which I had received from that excitable gentleman, which I passed across to my friend.

Holmes listened to my narrative with a quite extra-ordinary expression on his face and shook his head in disbelief as he read the letter. He put it down at last and gazed at me for a moment without speaking. 'Good old Watson!' he finally exclaimed, in affectionate exasperation. 'As always, running true to form! You have truly excelled yourself in this little affair and I must confess that I scarcely know whether to laugh or cry. You diligently took note of every fact of consequence — every fact except the most vital one of all, which was confronting you from the outset.'

'Now see here, Holmes!' I began, jumping indignantly to my feet, but there came an unexpected interruption. The door burst open, a protesting Mrs Hudson being elbowed contemptuously aside, and in strode the formidable figure of Mrs Crisparkle. 'Mr Holmes,' she cried, 'if ever a fiend walked the face of the earth in human form, that creature was John Jasper!'

'Capital!' exclaimed Holmes in delight, rubbing his hands in eager anticipation. 'At last we are getting somewhere! Mrs Crisparkle, please be seated. Mrs Hudson, some tea for our visitor.'

14

Helena Crisparkle, her face burning with passion, loosened her coat and sat down. 'I apologize', said she, after a moment, 'for what may have been my rather unconventional entry, but my blood boils whenever I think of that reptile. I must control myself. Thank you for your telegram, Mr Holmes. My husband and I came to London as soon as we received it. We are staying at the Strand Hotel. I left Septimus in our rooms and came straight here, for I can sometimes speak more freely in his absence – I have done so already, in fact! He is a wonderful man and understands much, but I sometimes fear that my outspokenness shocks him a little. Mr Holmes, how can I help you? And, even more to the point, how can you help *me*?'

By way of explanation, my companion had silently passed across the table to me, while Mrs Crisparkle was speaking, a copy of the telegram which he had sent to Cloisterham earlier that day. 'Neville Landless,' it ran. 'Do you still wish to clear his name? If so, I am at your disposal. Sherlock Holmes.'

'Thank you for coming,' he said now. 'I trust that you will

be able to clarify matters, Mrs Crisparkle, to our mutual benefit. There is no rush. Tell me, in your own words, about yourself and Neville.'

'Neville and I were twins,' she began, 'and the bond between us was thus far stronger, I think, than that between most brothers and sisters. We looked alike to some extent and we thought alike to a large extent. There were times, indeed, when there was an almost telepathic communication between us. Our childhood in Ceylon was, I fear, an extremely unhappy one and our education was shamefully neglected. I will not trouble you with the details. Suffice it to say that we came to England hoping to make a fresh start in life. Through the agency of a philanthropic society, we were both sent to Cloisterham — Neville being domiciled with Septimus (then a Minor Canon) and his mother, the intention being that he should carry out his studies under Septimus's supervision, and a place for myself being found at the Nuns' House seminary.

'Septimus and his mother, with the best of motives, had arranged a small dinner party at Minor Canon Corner as a means of welcoming us both to Cloisterham — but it proved to be, alas, one of the most fateful and horrible evenings of our lives. The guests included John Jasper, Edwin Drood, Rosa Bud, who was another pupil at the seminary, and Miss Twinkleton, the principal of that establishment.'

'And what did you make of Edwin Drood?' enquired Holmes.

'This was the one and only occasion that I ever encountered him, so it is unfair to form a judgement on such a limited acquaintance. He was a cheerful enough young man but perhaps inclined to be slightly too free with his opinions. Something of an extrovert, I would say.'

'And what do you think Mr Drood made of yourself?'

Our visitor seemed rather surprised at this unexpected question. 'Really, Mr Holmes,' she exclaimed, colouring afresh, 'I haven't the faintest idea. He addressed two or three remarks to me, and seemed gallant enough in his general attitude, but I was chiefly conscious of the fact that he was surprisingly patronizing towards Miss Bud, to whom he was supposed (albeit in an unofficial capacity) to be betrothed.'

'And what did you think of *her*?'

Helena Crisparkle smiled, for the first time. 'She was a perfect dear,' she said. 'The prettiest little child that I ever met — for she was no more than seventeen at that time. It was impossible to be in her company for long and not be attracted to her. Neville, I know, was most certainly smitten, and he was inclined to resent, in his rather hot-headed fashion, young Drood's cavalier attitude towards her.'

'And what, finally, did you make of Mr Jasper?'

The smile instantly disappeared. 'He was', she said, 'a handsome, courteous and extremely intelligent man but the most cold-blooded, calculating and repellent of creatures that I have ever encountered. It may well be, of course, that my opinion has been coloured by subsequent events, but even on that very first evening I soon realized (although, amazingly, nobody else did) that he was intensely interested in Rosa and that he wanted, above all things, to make her his own. He observed her from afar with a cool, calculating eye, with the air of one who bided his time. He was her music-master and when she was prevailed upon to sing he accompanied her at the piano in the most sinister, domineering of fashions, exercising so strange and tight a control over his pupil (especially when she seemed in danger of wandering from the tune) that she eventually broke down in tears. She confessed to me, later that night, that she was terrified of him. I find it incredible, even now, that no one else at that party – not Septimus, not Neville, and definitely not Mr Drood, who regarded his uncle with great affection – was aware of the extent to which he virtually mesmerized her and the horrible passion that he evidently felt.' And she shuddered at the recollection. 'Rosa herself', she added, 'did not fully realize, at that time, the extent of his obsession, although it would soon be made brutally clear to her.'

Mrs Hudson entered at this point, bearing cups of tea and a telegram for Holmes. He perused it, his face remaining impassive, then pushed it to one side.

'I imagine, Mr Holmes,' Mrs Crisparkle continued, sipping her tea, 'that you know something of what happened later on that first evening. Neville and Edwin Drood escorted Rosa, Miss Twinkleton and myself back to the seminary, but the moment we parted a row developed between them on the subject of Mr Drood's almost contemptuous treatment of Rosa. Jasper chanced upon them, just as they were coming to blows, and insisted that they both return with him to the gatehouse in an attempt to restore amicable relations. In the event, however, relations became far worse — deliberately enflamed, Neville later concluded, by something that Mr Jasper had added to both the young men's drinks — and passions reached such a sorry pitch that Neville actually flung himself upon Drood and had to be hauled off by Mr Jasper, being thrust into the street as a consequence. From that moment, I fear, our hopes of a happy life in Cloisterham were doomed. Mr Drood returned to London the following morning and Mr Jasper lost no opportunity for proclaiming, far and wide — chiefly, indeed, through the medium of unwitting mouthpieces — that Neville Landless had tried to murder his "dear boy", that he feared for Mr Drood's safety on future occasions and that, in short, a wild animal was lodged at Minor Canon Corner. He even had the temerity to suggest to my future husband, on one occasion, that Septimus's own life was in danger.

'It was Septimus who was instrumental in bringing about a reconciliation between Neville and Mr Drood on Christmas Eve, at a dinner party at the gatehouse presided over by Mr Jasper himself, and my brother returned to his lodgings convinced that all would be well between them in future. Deliberately absenting himself from the scene, for fear that his presence would otherwise cast a blight on sundry festive gatherings, he set out on a walking tour early the following morning. He had gone only a few miles, however, before he found himself pursued and taken prisoner by a gang of men who bore him back to Cloisterham, accused of the murder of Mr Drood. It was only the absence of a body that prevented him from being brought to trial.

'Thereafter, of course, it was impossible for Neville to remain in Cloisterham. Every man's hand was against him and Jasper was instrumental in ensuring that he was treated like a leper of old. Branded as a murderer, he eventually moved to London and took up lodgings in rooms found for him by Mr Grewgious, Rosa's guardian. Here he endeavoured to continue his studies, and Septimus looked in from time to time to see how he was faring. I joined him there myself a little while later and you may have observed, gentlemen, when you visited the Deanery, a little sketch that I made of him then. Even here, however, he was not safe from Mr Jasper, who pursued him with the implacable fury of an avenging angel and eventually caused it to be generally known that a Murderer was living in that particular tenement building.'

'You say "eventually",' interposed Holmes. 'There was, then, a short delay between Mr Jasper ascertaining your brother's whereabouts and his generally sounding an alarm in the neighbourhood. Would you be able to account for that delay?'

Helena's face looked troubled. 'It was, I fear, the execution of a threat,' she explained. 'Mr Jasper called upon Rosa one day that summer, when the pupils and most of the staff at the Nuns' House seminary were away, and threatened that he would, in effect, pursue Neville to the bitter end unless she agreed to surrender herself to him. He made this threat, you understand, not because there was a relationship of any kind between Neville and Rosa — for they had met only on that one occasion — but because he was the brother of someone of whom Rosa was very fond. It

131

was blackmail of the vilest kind.'

'So the proposition was, as you understand it, that Neville would remain unmolested if Rosa undertook to sacrifice herself in marriage to Mr Jasper?'

Helena nodded. 'The poor lamb, scarcely able to comprehend what hideous passions she had awakened in this monster, fled to London without delay and flung herself, understandably, upon her guardian for protection. Mr Grewgious, who had already had strong cause to revise his earlier good opinion of John Jasper, took control of the situation. He initially found her rooms in a nearby hotel – Wood's Hotel, on the north side of Furnival's Inn – and she stayed there for a short time, but Jasper was observed lurking near its entrance on more than one occasion and Mr Grewgious subsequently arranged for her to go into lodgings in Clerkenwell, some little distance away, with Miss Twinkleton to act as her temporary companion.

'Neville, in the mean time, became steadily more depressed. He worked hard at his studies, never venturing out except at night, but eventually became increasingly subject to acute melancholia. A Mr Tartar, a gentleman whom he had encountered in these lodgings (by a strange chance, my husband's old fag), was originally well disposed towards him, and a friendly face at a time like this was a boon indeed, but Mr Tartar gradually became somewhat cold in his attitude – reserving judgement, as it were, but indicating that he had distinct doubts about my brother's innocence. There may have been a slight tinge of jealousy so far as Rosa was concerned – although my brother and

Rosa never came into contact, despite their relatively close proximity for a short while — but I cannot help suspecting that Mr Jasper found some insidious means of working his poison. The loss of Mr Tartar's comradeship was a determining factor in plunging Neville further into depression. He eventually moved to Lincoln, accompanied by myself, in the hope of lying low until the mystery concerning Edwin Drood was brought to a head, but even here John Jasper managed to pursue him. That man, Mr Holmes, was possessed of a demoniacal energy — it often seemed that he had perfected the art of being in two places at once! Once again, word got around that there was a murderer in the city and Neville found himself shunned by his new neighbours. Like Cain, he was treated as a fugitive and vagabond on the face of the earth.

'Our hope', she continued, 'that the mystery of Mr Drood's disappearance might be resolved at an early date was not entirely without foundation. A friend of Mr Grewgious, who had been keeping John Jasper under careful observation for several months past —'

'One moment. This friend of Mr Grewgious. It would be Mr Datchery, I assume?'

'That's right.'

'And Mr Grewgious had sent him to Cloisterham, I take it, for the express purpose of watching John Jasper?'

'Not exactly,' she said, frowning. 'I never met Mr Datchery myself, but I have the impression that he came out of the blue, as it were, and offered his services to Mr Grewgious of his own accord. I do not believe that they had been previously acquainted. It may be that he was a distant connection of Bazzard, Mr Grewgious's clerk -- a most peculiar man, so I gather, but one who moved in theatrical circles -- but this is mere surmise.'

'I see. Pray continue.'

'Mr Datchery, as I say, had been keeping Mr Jasper under careful observation and had also made diligent enquiry into his activities during the months immediately preceding Edwin Drood's disappearance. He formed the conclusion that Jasper had himself murdered his nephew and hidden his body somewhere in the churchyard -- immured, in all probability, in quicklime, so that there would be virtually nothing left of him. The removal of the watch and shirt-pin, which would have been identifying features in view of their known resistance to the properties of quicklime, certainly suggested this. He also suspected that Mr Jasper had somehow gained access to the Sapsea tomb and had secreted the body in the spot reserved for our worthy mayor. You will think me, I fear, incredibly cold-blooded to be sitting here calmly narrating these conclusions without turning a hair, but you must remember that I have been familiar with this tale for more than a quarter of a century and it long ago lost its power to shock.'

'Not at all,' said Holmes. 'Please go on.'

'Mr Grewgious's friend, shortly before he left the area (for reasons I never could ascertain), had devised a plan whereby Jasper was to be startled into confessing his guilt. On the night that he disappeared Edwin was carrying, on his person, a ring which he had originally intended to present to Rosa as a means of marking their formal betrothal — it was of great sentimental value, having belonged originally to Rosa's mother, and it was only with great reluctance that Mr Grewgious (who had developed misgivings about the advisability of the match) parted with it to Edwin. In the event, however, Edwin and Rosa agreed of their own accord that they should not proceed with their engagement and Edwin had retained it, presumably intending to return it to Mr Grewgious's safe-keeping. The person responsible for murdering Edwin, however, while removing his gold watch, its chain and his shirt-pin, would not have been aware that a valuable ring, quite distinct in its appearance and instantly identifiable, was also secreted about the body.

'Mr Datchery's plan, therefore, was that Mr Grewgious should casually inform John Jasper, a day or so before Christmas 1870, that Rosa Bud had become engaged to another (a Mr Jack Tartar) and that it was a thousand pities that she could not wear her mother's engagement ring, which Edwin had had in his possession when he disappeared. It was surmised that this would be startling news to Mr Jasper, especially in view of the fact that Mr Sapsea was no longer a young man and might be joining his wife in the family tomb before very much longer, and that — in short, that John Jasper would hurry along to the churchyard and seek to retrieve the ring from what, if anything, remained of his nephew's body.' And at this point, despite her earlier brave words, Mrs Crisparkle's voice faltered and she was unable to repress a shudder.

'Take your time, Mrs Crisparkle, there is no hurry.'

She swallowed, and then continued. 'The plan was, briefly, that just as John Jasper reached the point where he had last seen the body, and was about to search for the ring, a young man who to all intents and purposes *was* Edwin Drood, clad in clothes identical to those which Drood had been wearing when last seen in the land of the living, would step out and silently confront him. Mr Jasper, so it was thought, would then break down and confess his guilt.'

'And where was this duplicate Edwin Drood to come from?' asked Holmes.

'The intention had been that Neville should play that role. He had been familiar with the clothes and hat that Edwin had been wearing on that fateful evening, was of approximately the same age and build and would have been quite capable, for a few moments, of convincing Jasper that he was gazing upon the spectre of the murdered man. Mr Grewgious, Mr Tartar, Lobley (Mr Tartar's man) and Septimus would then have emerged from their sundry places of concealment and apprehended him.' She paused, reflectively, for a few minutes and gazed unseeingly at the wall.

'But all did not go according to plan?' suggested Holmes.

Mrs Crisparkle shook her head. 'Neville', she said bitterly, 'was struck down by a brainstorm on 22 December – exactly twenty-five years ago today, in fact – and died within minutes. He was John Jasper's second victim, Mr Holmes, for that swine had hounded him – or been responsible for others hounding him – until he could endure no longer. He died like a beast at bay, totally innocent of any crime, but pursued from pillar to post until he could go on no longer.'

There was a moment's silence. 'I was aware of this,' said Holmes gently, at length. 'I ascertained from Somerset House, earlier today, the time, place and cause of his death. So the plan had to be abandoned, then?'

Helena Crisparkle shook her head. 'Oh no!' she cried vehemently. 'Not for the world! If there had been cause before why we should hunt John Jasper down and thrust him into the condemned cell, there was double the cause now. The plan went ahead.'

'And the young man?'

'Was myself. Don't look so surprised, Mr Holmes! It was not the first time that I had dressed up in boy's clothes, although it was certainly the last.'

'I have had some experience', said Holmes, smiling at the recollection, 'of another young lady who did precisely the same thing. But I am interrupting. Please continue.'

'It all went horribly wrong,' said Mrs Crisparkle bitterly. 'On the first night, nothing happened. On the second night, 24 December, Mr Jasper did indeed come stealing into the churchyard, holding a dark lantern, and he made straight for the Sapsea tomb. He paused a moment, apparently searching for something about his person, and I stepped out to confront him. But instead of breaking down and confessing all, as we had innocently expected, he broke out into an exultant cry of delight. "So, Landless," he snarled, "the old adage is correct — murderers *do* return to the scene of the crime! At last, I have you!" He flung himself upon me and the next moment his hands were around my throat. He

137

was totally convinced in that instant, not only that I was my brother (of whose death he was evidently unaware) but that Neville was indeed the murderer of Edwin Drood. We fell to the ground, but now that we were at close quarters he realized his terrible mistake — that it was a woman he was trying to strangle, not a man — and the next instant Tartar and Lobley were upon us and pulling him free. His rage, mixed with his disappointment, was awesome to behold — he collapsed in a heap, foaming at the mouth, and we found ourselves calling for medical assistance instead of the local constabulary. It transpired (though I cannot express any regrets) that his mind was permanently unhinged and we heard, later, that he had been committed to an asylum. The rest you know.

'So the matter, Mr Holmes, never was resolved. John Jasper, far from confessing his guilt, had evidently believed, during those frightful few minutes, that he was grappling with the murderer of his beloved nephew. But I am equally convinced, whatever the world might say, that my poor, dear brother could not have been responsible for the death of Mr Drood. If you can indeed clear his name, then I will be everlastingly in your debt.'

There was a moment's silence. 'I blame myself to some extent,' she continued, in a dull, colourless, ruminating voice. 'I had, unfortunately, only seen Edwin Drood on that one occasion and I obviously bore a far greater resemblance to Neville than I did to Mr Drood. Yet I cannot help thinking, strange though it is, that if only Mr Datchery had not gone away things might have worked out differently. Although I never met that gentleman, he appears to have possessed an unerring touch for overcoming difficulties. Without him, the rest of us — myself, Mr Grewgious, Mr Tartar, Mr Lobley, Septimus and even Rosa — were bereft of a guiding force that might have made all the difference. It could be said, perhaps, that we were six characters in need of a stage-manager! Mr Grewgious was a good, kind man, extremely resourceful and capable, yet he somehow lacked the force, the guiding purpose required, to seize control of the situation and see it through to the bitter end. But these', she said, wrenching herself out of her mood of abstraction, 'are foolish fancies, Mr Holmes, and I am wasting your time.'

'Not at all, not at all. And what happened to you all after this unfortunate outcome to your little scheme?'

She laughed rather bitterly. 'In essence,' she said, 'we went our separate ways, for there was nothing to hold us together any more. Rosa married Mr Tartar some months later and I returned to Cloisterham, teaching at Miss Twinkleton's seminary for a time until Septimus did me the honour of making me his wife.'

'And you lost contact with Rosa and her husband?'

'Yes, for all practical purposes. My relations with Mr Tartar had become, as you will have gathered, somewhat strained, for Neville's innocence remained unproven and Mr Tartar had seen no reason — especially in the light of what took place in the churchyard that night — to banish his doubts on that matter.'

'So you haven't seen or heard from Rosa for twenty-five years?'

'No, I haven't seen her but we communicate occasionally

— and I wrote to her, of course, when her husband died.'

'Indeed!' said Holmes, sitting up. 'And when was this?'

'Oh, seven or eight months ago now — there was a small item in the *Telegraph* to the effect that Mr Jack Tartar had been killed in a climbing accident in the Swiss Alps, and I immediately sent Rosa my commiserations. I had a brief line in response.'

'I would be grateful,' said Holmes, 'if you could supply me with Mrs Tartar's current address. It is imperative that I see her without delay.'

Mrs Crisparkle promised to send a messenger to Baker Street with this information the following morning, adding that Rosa was living somewhere in Bournemouth.

'One final question,' said Holmes. 'You mentioned, a little while ago, that sketch (and a very evocative one it is too!) which you made of your brother. We could not help observing, when we had the pleasure of lunching at the Deanery last Christmas, that there was a remarkably fine portrait of yourself hanging alongside it. I wonder if you could tell me who the artist was?'

Mrs Crisparkle looked at my friend in some surprise. 'I cannot recall his name,' she said. 'It was done many years ago, soon after the events which we have just been discussing and at a time, indeed, when I would much have preferred a period of seclusion. The young man in question was a penniless French refugee (for this was at the time of the Franco-Prussian war) and Mr Grewgious had taken upon himself the role of patron. Mr Grewgious was anxious to obtain some commissions for the young gentleman and the painting served, indeed, as a wedding present from him to Septimus and myself.'

'Thank you,' said Holmes. 'You have been immensely helpful. There are no further questions but I would be grateful if you and the Dean could delay your return to Cloisterham for a day or so. Ideally, I know, the Dean would wish to be there on Christmas Eve, but I have the feeling that events of great moment are upon us and I would wish you to remain close at hand for a little while longer. There are at least two visits that Watson and I need to make, with Bournemouth being our first port of call, and our investigation will then, I trust, be complete.'

Mrs Crisparkle willingly consented to my friend's request. 'One final word,' she said, as she rose to take her leave. 'It was never officially established that John Jasper was responsible for the death of Edwin Drood, and I must confess that, after the lapse of so many years, I no longer greatly care whether it is or not. What I do know, however, is that he was responsible for besmirching the memory of my dear brother, as well as for his death, and that is something about which I still care very much indeed.'

'If the record can be put straight,' said Holmes, 'then rest assured that it most certainly will be – and the pen of my colleague, here, will be primarily responsible for ensuring that, sooner or later, the public are made fully aware of what befell Mr Drood and at whose door the blame for his disappearance should be laid.'

Warmly acknowledging this potential commission, and pledging myself to discharge it to the best of my ability, I escorted Mrs Crisparkle downstairs to the waiting cab.

141

When I returned to our quarters Holmes held out to me, without a word, the telegram delivered earlier. It was from James Wakefield and stated that Mr John Jasper had made an 'unauthorized departure' from Stazeby Nanton.

15

That night, the heavens opened. The sound of intense rain drumming on the roof rendered sleep almost impossible and I managed, in the event, no more than a troubled doze, wondering, from time to time, whether Mr Jasper was likely to pay another visit to Baker Street and, if so, whether there would be a sudden thunderous hammering at the door of No. 221b.

There was indeed an early-morning visitor and at the sound of the rat-a-tat-tat I leaped out of bed and was half-way down the stairs only to find that Holmes was there before me, that Mrs Hudson was there before us both and that the caller in question, water streaming from his cape, was simply a lad from the Strand Hotel who had brought round the details of Rosa Tartar's address from Mrs Crisparkle. He was amply rewarded for his pains and splashed his way back to the hotel. The rain continued to stream down incessantly.

'Scarcely the weather', said Holmes, 'for a trip to the south coast, and I must confess — when all is said and done — that the points that Mrs Tartar will be able to clarify, in the light of what we learnt last night, are now unlikely to be of more than marginal importance. But she is the last of our witnesses — or, at all events, *almost* the last — and it is imperative that we see her without delay. Are you game for an out-of-season trip to Bournemouth, Watson? I fancy that oilskins and galoshes will be required!'

I confirmed that I was, as ever, fully prepared to accompany my friend wherever he wished. As soon as breakfast was concluded, and appropriately armed against the foulest of foul weathers, we were in a cab heading for Waterloo Station. Arriving there in an acutely wet condition, we caught the first available train and slowly steamed our way towards the south-west. The rain continued to pelt down in a monotonous torrent and we made but sluggish progress. I had bought a copy of the *Daily Graphic* at the station bookstall, with a view to familiarizing myself with the latest dispatches from its special military correspondent in Cuba, while Holmes, as was his wont, had purchased a large collection of newspapers of every description, which he skimmed through with no great patience. 'Ha!' he exclaimed at one point, after perusing the drama critic of the *Saturday Review*. 'If we wish to familiarize ourselves with the spectacle of a young soprano under the spell of a mesmerist, a visit to the Haymarket in the not too distant future may prove instructive — for Tree, I note, is essaying the role of Svengali.'

'Also instructive in this context,' he added thoughtfully, a little while later, after tossing the last of his papers to one side, 'is the strange story of what befell that Scottish member of your profession some ten years back. There are, it seems, precedents for virtually everything, although problems of identification are such that it is sometimes difficult to say which of them actually came first.' He was lost in thought for some little time, gazing from the window at the rain-swept landscape. 'It is certainly not inconceivable,' he added whimsically, 'that Gaelic mists might drift as far as the south of England, though whether they could be wafted across the Channel to Gaul, despite the obvious affinity, is another matter.' And then, after an even longer silence: 'One might conclude, I suppose, that the Scottish Queen has much to answer for!'

I had found it difficult to follow Holmes's train of thought and could not see, for the life of me, what Mary Queen of Scots had to do with our investigations. But he had murmured these final inconsequential words so drowsily that it was clear that he too had passed a troubled night, with only fitful slumbers, and that loss of sleep was finally making itself felt. This seemed to be confirmed, a little while later, when he slipped into a doze.

I stared, through the streaming windows, at the leaden, sullen landscape through which we were slowly making our way, much enveloped in mist, and reflected on the whole strange story of the Edwin Drood saga, which had now had us embroiled for almost exactly a year. I must have nodded off in my own turn, for the next thing I knew was that a tremendous screeching of brakes, and expulsion of steam, were proclaiming the fact that we had finally reached the end of our journey and had arrived at Bournemouth. Scrambling down, to be greeted by the incessant drumming of rain on the roof of the station, we eventually hired a cab and clattered off, through monumental puddles, to Voredale Towers, a residence located in Wenskerry Gardens.

The cab dropped us at the gates and we squelched our way up the drive, our umbrellas proving a sadly inadequate protection against what had developed into a howling tornado of a storm. I was much impressed by the size of the house, for it was nothing less than a small mansion. 'Mrs Tartar', murmured Holmes as he pulled the bellrope, and noting my surprise, 'is now a very wealthy lady. Quite apart from whatever funds the late Mr Tartar may have left her, she inherited a substantial sum from her parents and also, for that matter, from Mr Grewgious, a bachelor gentleman who seems to have regarded her as his own daughter.'

The door was opened by a maid, who noted our bedraggled condition with a certain degree of sympathy but was obviously loath to invite us inside. 'Is your mistress at home?' enquired Holmes. 'We have travelled a considerable distance, on a matter of some urgency, and would be grateful if Mrs Tartar could spare us a little of her time.'

'Oh no, sir!' exclaimed the girl. 'The mistress is away for a few days – I can't rightly say when she'll be back, I'm afraid.'

But at this point there was a call of 'Who is it, Edith?' and a very good-looking young lady appeared in the hall. I was almost certain (but hesitated to mention the fact, for fear of proving mistaken) that she was the girl whose 'Morning Glory' portrait I had admired at the Royal Academy some five months before.

'Miss Florence Tartar, I believe?' exclaimed Holmes. 'My name is Sherlock Holmes and this is my colleague, Dr

Watson. We are very anxious for a brief interview with your mother in connection with some happenings many years ago which have never been satisfactorily resolved.'

'Do come in, gentlemen,' said the self-possessed young woman, her eyes sparkling with interest. She led us through to the drawing-room. 'You're too late for lunch, I am afraid, but perhaps I can interest you in some sherry?' (She could indeed.) 'I'm very familiar with your name and reputation, Mr Holmes — fancy Mamma being involved in one of your cases! This is certainly going to liven up a soggy old day. And how wet you are!' A few minutes later, however, she was pouting with vexation as Holmes explained, regretfully, that it was a confidential matter on which he wanted to see Mrs Tartar, that he was not at liberty to reveal any of the details and that he would be greatly obliged if he could be informed of Mrs Tartar's whereabouts.

'Oh, that's not fair!' exclaimed our young hostess. 'You want me to tell *you* something but you won't tell *me* anything in return. I'll throw you out into the rain without further ado unless you give me at least a hint of what it's all about.'

Holmes, unaccustomed to playful exchanges of this fashion, breathed rather heavily. 'Miss Tartar,' he said at length, 'have you ever heard your mother refer to a Mr Edwin Drood?'

She shook her head.

'Or to a Mr John Jasper?'

Again, a shake of the pretty head.

'Then I fear I am unable to elucidate further. As I say, our visit concerns matters which happened many years ago and

147

if your mother has not seen fit to enlighten you concerning these gentlemen then it seems best that I emulate her example. Miss Tartar, I wish you a very good afternoon.'

He bowed and then made for the door, with myself following suit, but there came a petulant cry of 'Stop!' from the young lady. 'You really are', she said, 'the most provoking of men that I have ever encountered. You arrive here out of the blue (in a figurative sense), mention the names of some strange people that I have never heard of, arouse my interest in my mother's early life, about which I know virtually nothing, and then take your leave without a single word of proper explanation. What have I to do with your Edwin Droods or John Jaspers?' And she stamped her foot in annoyance.

Holmes waited patiently until she had finished. 'I am sorry,' he said at length, 'but the secrets are not mine to divulge. If you are unable to inform us of your mother's whereabouts, then our visit is at an end.'

'Oh, very well,' she said crossly. 'Mother has gone to London for two or three days. There! Now you know.'

'She is staying with friends, presumably?'

'No, she's gone to a hotel, but you'd never guess which one. It's nowhere near the West End or the bright lights, where all the exciting things happen and the best people are, but it's stuck in that frowsty, dry-as-dust, legal part of the City, where they have all those Inns and gentlemen rushing about in long gowns and short wigs and silly things like that.'

Holmes stiffened. 'That would be Wood's Hotel, I believe?'

'That's right! How clever of you. A funny little place, and very off the beaten track, but Mamma always stops there on her visits to London – not that she makes many, you understand. I think it has a sentimental attachment for her – she was staying there when she first met my father.'

'Miss Tartar, I am much indebted to you,' said Holmes, and this time we really did take our leave. The young lady, her curiosity unsatisfied as her day's excitement came to an end, saw us reluctantly to the door. We emerged into the same torrential downpour and, there being no cab at hand, were obliged to walk to the station. A local train took us to Mugsby Junction. Here we found that there would be a wait of forty minutes for the next train to London but this break in our journey did enable us, at any rate, to fortify ourselves at the refreshments room.

Holmes ate the unappetizing sandwiches with no great enthusiasm and looked frequently at his watch. 'You will appreciate, of course,' he said, 'the reason for my unease. Mr Jasper, so we learnt last night, was detected "lurking" in the vicinity of Wood's Hotel on two or three occasions when Rosa Bud was staying there. It does not follow, of course, that he will go there on this occasion, assuming that he somehow contrives to make his way to London, and nor does it follow that he would necessarily recognize the lady in question after a lapse of twenty-five years. But stranger things have happened already in this curious tale!'

Little more did he say for the moment. Our journey was unduly protracted and I was aware, every time that the train halted or slowed down, of his mounting impatience. By early evening we were back in London – finding, to our great relief, that the rain had finally eased — and in a cab heading for Wood's Hotel in Furnival's Inn. It was indeed, as Miss Florence had described it, off the beaten track and by the time we had alighted from our conveyance the darkened streets were almost deserted.

Wood's Hotel, used chiefly for the accommodation of court case witnesses obliged to stay in town overnight, was unassuming to the point of being positively unprepossessing. The receptionist, from his poorly lit cubicle, peered out at us in some surprise.

'Have you a Mrs Tartar among your guests?' Holmes enquired.

The receptionist shook his head emphatically but slowly moved his ink-stained finger down the hotel register. 'No sir,' he firmly announced at length, with an air of triumph. 'We have no Mrs Tartar.' And he slammed the book shut.

'Could she be using her maiden name, I wonder? Have you a Miss Rosa Bud staying here?'

The receptionist raised his eyebrows. 'Ah, that's a different matter,' he responded, without pausing to consult his register. 'Room 18 on the first floor. You're her second visitor this evening, sir,' he added. 'A gentleman went up to see her not five minutes since.'

Holmes, without another word, and much to the clerk's astonishment, bounded up the stairs two at a time, with myself in hot pursuit. He raced along the shabby, ill-lit corridor, peering at the numbers on each of the doors, and eventually flung open that of Room 18. There were two people in the room, a man and a woman sitting close together by the fireside, who started up in bewilderment

150

and alarm as Holmes burst in. 'A thousand apologies for this interruption,' he exclaimed, but with a note of intense relief in his voice.

'Monsieur Dupont!' exclaimed I, close upon his heels, in astonishment.

Holmes shook his head. 'Not quite,' said he, with a smile. 'Allow me to introduce you, Watson, to Mr Edwin Drood.'

16

A few minutes later, with the briefest of introductions and explanations having been effected and with the hotel management having been prevailed upon to provide some liquid refreshments, Holmes and I drew up two chairs of our own to that fireside. Mrs Tartar, now, alas, a rather full-blown rose but a cheerful little woman with a twinkle in her eye, made us both very welcome, bustled about whenever the need to refill our glasses arose, and beamed upon all three of us in the happiest of manners. M. Dupont, as I still found myself thinking of him, had dispensed with the pince-nez and seemed altogether less foreign (and even slightly taller) as he sprawled at his ease in a comfortable armchair. He seemed, rather to my surprise, totally unconcerned by the fact that his true identity had now been revealed.

'My apologies, Dr Watson,' he began, with an affable smile,' for that altercation in Peckham a few months ago. I hammed it up unmercifully, I'm afraid, but it's a trick that I've often had to resort to as a means of getting rid of unwelcome or awkward visitors. When you started mentioning Miss Rosa Bud I began to realize that my past was catching up with me, and no mistake! Having not the faintest idea who you were, a quick exit seemed prudent.'

'My friend noticed', said Holmes, 'that your English was very poor, but had he been much longer in your company I suspect that he would scarcely have failed to perceive that your French was even worse.'

The artist cheerfully confessed that this would indeed have been the case. 'The months I spent in Paris', he said, 'certainly helped me to pick up some of the lingo, and I can manage the odd phrase or two without too much difficulty, but the smattering which I acquired during that period has now almost left me. A genuine Frog would spot that I was an impostor in an instant.'

'In recent months,' said Holmes genially, his glass having been refilled by the busy little woman, 'I must confess that I have been taking a keen interest in the works of M. Dupont.'

This was news to me, for I had had no reason to suppose that my friend had even heard of the artist prior to our conversation of the previous morning. 'I was not aware, Holmes,' I interposed, somewhat stiffly, 'that you were an expert on the French Impressionist school of painting.'

My companion chuckled. 'Now that,' he said, 'I cannot lay claim to. But did it not occur to you, my dear chap, that it was remarkable that Mr Edwin Drood and M. Edmund Dupont should bear the same initials? By what was, I must acknowledge, pure chance, I happened to see in Cloisterham on the Christmas Day of last year, within the space of a very few hours, two portraits. One of them was a poorly executed daub of a pretty young girl; another was a brilliant depiction of a striking young woman. Both very different in

153

style, yet they had one feature in common. In the bottom right-hand corner of the more accomplished production there appeared, in very tiny print, the initials E.D. The other was unsigned but had been executed, so I discovered, by Mr Jasper's nephew. The portrait of Miss Landless was clearly not the work of an untrained amateur. I ascertained that the only portrait painter of any repute in this country bearing the initials E.D. and (for my purposes) of approximately the right age, was a certain Edmund Dupont. On a recent visit to Paris I made some discreet enquiries about the origins of this M. Dupont and discovered that he was completely unknown in what purported to be his native land.

'But it was not until yesterday morning,' he continued, addressing himself directly to the artist, 'when my good friend Watson showed me a note you had sent him, that my suspicions were finally confirmed. A comparison between the writing of M. Dupont, in October 1895, with what I recalled of the writing of Mr Drood in December 1869, proved extremely instructive! There was also', he added reflectively, 'another Frenchman bearing the initials E.D. who came to mind – and, indeed, another Edmund – who masqueraded as a Count, if I mistake not, as a means of revisiting the scenes of his youth undetected. But *that* Edmund played, I believe, a rather more active role than *this* one!'

'You're quite right, Mr Holmes,' the portrait painter acknowledged. 'Edwin Drood, for all practical purposes, came to an end twenty-six years ago and Edmund Dupont has been content, by and large, to lead a totally separate existence. Apart from anything else, nature intended me to be an artist rather than an engineer, but having assumed an identity more congenial to me than my previous one, and taking all the factors into account, it seemed the most prudent course of all to keep things as they were.'

'You must remember', said Holmes, 'that I am not yet acquainted with all the factors in this case. You are certainly under no compulsion to tell me anything at all, M. Dupont (since this is the persona you prefer), but I feel that, even at this late hour, it could still do some positive good if the true story were revealed once and for all. While uncertainty remains, I fear that there are several quarters in which unhappiness still prevails.'

'Go on, Eddy,' urged the little lady. 'It can certainly do no harm, after all these years, and — as Mr Holmes says — some good may still come of it.'

'And confession', acknowledged M. Dupont, 'is good for the soul. Not that I have much to confess, mind you! I may have assumed an identity that was not my own, but it wasn't anybody else's either. Anyway, now that you have tracked me down, gentlemen (and I seem to have given you a pretty good run for your money), you must hear my tale and judge for yourselves.'

I did not find his flippant manner altogether agreeable, and I wondered whether he fully appreciated just how much trouble had been created by his failure to proclaim that he was alive and well. As his story unfolded, however, I gradually inclined to the opinion that his careless approach was, to some extent, yet another mask, and one that had been adopted as a means of hiding a fundamental insecurity. The little woman, at any rate, saw nothing to complain of in his attitude, and hung upon his every word with rapt attention.

'I am not sure, Mr Holmes,' he began, 'how much you already know about that terrible Christmas Eve twenty-six years ago. You will presumably be aware that there had been bad relations between myself and Neville Landless for several weeks and that Mr Crisparkle was primarily responsible for seeking to bring about a reconciliation between us. My uncle, John Jasper, played host to us at the gatehouse that night and things went, in the circumstances, far better than could have been expected. Both Landless and I were on our best behaviour towards each other and a genuine amicability appeared to be established between us. A fantastic storm raged throughout the evening, although dying out towards midnight, and when the time came for Landless to return to Minor Canon Corner it was suggested, although I'm not too clear whose idea it was, that before he and I went to our respective slumbers we should stroll down to the river to observe the extent to which it had overflowed its banks. Truth to tell, I had evidently drunk rather more than I ought to have done. The alcohol was having such a strange effect upon me that I thought it would be all to the good if I broke away from the rather too convivial atmosphere of the gatehouse and managed to shake off some of the fuzziness that was beginning to affect my wits.

'I walked down to the river with Landless and we gazed at the strangely unreal sight of the turbulent waters churning and slurping against the banks. The effects of the drink remained very strong, however, and everything

156

began to take on a strange, dreamlike quality – I heard my own voice, and that of my companion, coming from a long way off. There was a strange buzzing sensation in my ears and I appeared to be cushioned all around, like a man walking in a dream. I am under the impression that I returned, at length, to the gatehouse and said what was, to my own ears, a muffled goodbye to Landless. I leant against the door to regain my senses, with the world reeling about me, and a moment later was gripped by the arm. A distant voice said, 'Come, you do not seem well; we'll walk in the churchyard for a while. The night air will help to revive you.' My arm was taken and on we walked – or rather stumbled, in my case. I was steered towards the churchyard and was aware of the gravestones looming up. It was impossible to identify my companion. My senses were deadened and the buzzing in my ears became louder.

'The voice eventually commanded me to pause a moment and my arm was released. I suddenly found it exceedingly difficult to breathe and became aware that something was tightening around my throat. I struggled, feebly, to dislodge the mysterious something, but all in vain – I had no strength at all and felt myself falling into a pit. My senses virtually took leave of me, although I was dimly aware of a hand fumbling with my waistcoat. I realised, later, that my watch and shirt-pin were being removed at this point. Then I had the sensation that all was over and that I had been left alone. The fresh air was cut off, to be replaced by indescribable putrescent odours. A door closed and I heard, from afar, the sound of a key being turned. There was a roof over my head and dust in my mouth and I was cold, but all I wanted to do was to curl up and go to sleep in this claustrophobic, uncomfortable yet strangely soft, squelchy resting place. But a little while later – it might have been minutes, or it might have been hours – there came, once again, the sound of a key being turned and the next thing I knew was that I had been seized by the legs and dragged out, coughing and choking.'

'Like Belzoni from the ruins,' interposed the little lady.

'Like Belzoni from the ruins. It transpired, when I had returned (after a fashion) to my senses that my rescuer was the stonemason – Durdles, the queerest of old chaps but the most wonderful of life-savers – who had seen me being attacked from afar, had hidden until my assailant left the tomb into which I had been stuffed and then came to my rescue. He was joined, a few minutes later, by an appalling urchin of a boy and together they helped me to a strange little hovel of a dosshouse – the Travellers' Tuppenny, I believe they called it – where I did my best to wash away the hideous material in which my clothes and face were plastered (although I retain some scars to this very day, hence the beard) and rested a while to take stock of the situation.

'The situation was so incredible that I had difficulty in taking it in! It was unbelievable that somebody had made an attack upon me and actually tried to kill me, but I somehow forced myself, during the hours of that terrible night, to accept the inconceivable. My reason told me that it must be Landless, who had indeed made a physical attack upon me on one occasion – although I now have reason to believe that the quarrel between us had been largely fomented by my uncle – but I could not, even so, believe that it was truly he. We had spent the evening as friends and past enmities between us had appeared to be genuinely at an end. Yet if it was not Landless, it could only be Jack – and that, to me, was equally unbelievable. In short, Mr Holmes, I did not know which of them had done this thing! Durdles, alas, had been too far away to be able to identify my attacker. Not knowing what to think, and with my head reeling from the enormity of what had happened, I decided that the best thing I could do was to leave Cloisterham instantly and to seek counsel with wiser heads than mine. Attired as a tramp – for, in the only spare set of clothes that the demon-child of the Travellers' Tuppenny was able to provide, I could not masquerade as anything else! – I returned to London and flung myself upon the protection of Mr Grewgious, Rosa's guardian.'

'And your rescuers?'

'Durdles and the boy were both sworn to silence. I made it my business to ensure, later, that Durdles was richly rewarded for his labours but I doubt, on the whole, whether the boy had much conception of what had actually happened. He appeared late on the scene, armed (incredibly!) with a handful of stones to hurl at Durdles as a way of encouraging him to go home, and was under the impression, I believe, that I was simply one of the stonemason's drinking companions who had met with some kind of an accident.'

'And why *was* the stonemason abroad at so late an hour of the day?'

'A curious tale, Mr Holmes, and one that I have never

been able to fathom. It seems that, on the *previous* Christmas Eve, the Christmas Eve of 1868 that is, Durdles was asleep in the churchyard in a drunken stupor at about that time and was awoken by what he described to me as the "ghost of a cry – the ghost of one terrific shriek". And that was followed, he claimed, by "the ghost of a howl of a dog – a long dismal woeful howl, such as a dog gives when a person's dead". But nobody else, according to Durdles, had heard these strange sounds, although he had enquired far and wide, and he had returned to the churchyard on *this* Christmas Eve to see whether they would be repeated.'

'A night-shriek,' said Holmes with interest, 'and followed by a howl. Singular indeed! If wolves still roamed abroad in this part of the world, to serve as a murderer's sentinel, an explanation might, perhaps, come to mind. But this is Kent in the nineteenth century, not Inverness in the eleventh, and we must banish such thoughts from our conjectures. Pray continue.'

'I went, as I said, to Mr Grewgious, who was astonished by my story. He decided that, until such time as further investigations could be carried out, and it had been clearly established whether Mr Landless, or Jack or even somebody else, had been responsible for this attempt on my life, it would be best if I disappeared from the scene completely. He considered that, for my own security, I should leave the country altogether and stay away until it was safe for me to reappear. We agreed that I should go to Paris, which seemed a pleasant enough destination, and that Bazzard, Mr Grewgious's clerk, should accompany me and act as my companion and bodyguard. Before the year 1869 had come

160

to its end, therefore, we had crossed the Channel and had taken up residence in the artists' quarter of the city. It was here that I had the golden opportunity to study the rudiments of painting and discover the true vocation of my life.'

'And Mr Bazzard was with you for the whole of this time?'

'He was indeed!' Dupont agreed enthusiastically. 'He proved a marvellous companion and we came through many an adventure together.'

'Just in passing,' said Holmes, 'and you must forgive me for this odd digression, do you have the slightest reason of any kind to suppose that Mr Bazzard — or even, indeed, yourself — was acquainted with an elderly gentleman called Dick Datchery, who took up residence in Cloisterham six or seven months after your disappearance?'

Dupont looked mystified. 'That's a new name to me,' he said. 'I certainly never knew anybody called Datchery and I doubt whether Bazzard did either — but I'll make a point of asking him.' (He did, and the answer proved to be a negative one.)

'So,' said Holmes, 'you had been saved from a dusty death, you took up residence in Paris and you became absorbed in painting. What followed?'

'What followed,' said Dupont with a grimace, 'was the Franco-Prussian war and the German siege of Paris — factors that had *not* been allowed for when I decided to take up residence there! Bazzard and I made our escape and eventually returned to England. By this time I had grown my beard and was virtually unrecognizable as the young

161

man who had left its shores some eighteen months before, but I thought I'd play safe by pretending to be a Frenchman until Bazzard had seen Mr Grewgious and ascertained how the land lay.'

'And how did it?'

'Not at all well, unfortunately. He discovered that Neville Landless was dead, that Uncle Jack was in an asylum and that the mystery of who had made that horrible attack upon me – and whether, in fact, he was still at large – was as much a mystery as ever. (It has remained a mystery ever since – to me, at any rate!) It seemed, one way and the other, decidedly inopportune for Edwin Drood to come back to life. No one would have been particularly glad to see me – and Rosa, I found, had married Jack Tartar, so that it might have been a mite embarrassing for her (formal disengagements notwithstanding!) if I had reappeared on the scene. This being so, I decided to retain the identity of Edmund Dupont, to pass myself off as a refugee and to try to earn my living as a portrait painter. Bazzard, having had some theatrical experience, was able to give me a few tips on how to build up my character as an eccentric Froggie and Mr Grewgious was instrumental, in the early days, in finding me one or two commissions.

'I was eventually able to establish myself and have made, though I say it myself, a fair success of my career. Whether I could have had the same success under an English name is another matter! Peckham seemed as good a place to settle down as anywhere if one wished to assume a new identity without attracting too much attention, and there I've been to this day. And Bazzard, when Mr Grewgious died, came to me as secretary. Until I heard, earlier this year, that Rosa had unfortunately become a widow, and rushed off to offer my condolences and resume our old friendship, the ghost of Edwin Drood had ne'er been seen in the land. I little thought, however, when I did that painting of her daughter (who looks now as her mother did twenty-five years ago) and had it accepted by the Royal Academy, that I would have Dr Watson knocking at my door!'

'I believe', Holmes suggested drily, 'that you are being slightly disingenuous in disclaiming any connection with your previous existence. Did you not return to Cloisterham on at least one occasion?'

Dupont, with a glance at Mrs Tartar, seemed vexed by this question. 'Yes, you know about that, of course,' he conceded ruefully. 'I must confess that Helena Landless had struck me, on the one occasion that I met her, as a fine figure of a woman and I had a strong desire to do her justice on canvas. I won't deny, in fact, that one or two other thoughts had also occurred to me, and I persuaded Mr Grewgious, against his better judgement, to introduce me to her in the character of an artist. I had had some idea of revealing my true identity, if things showed any signs of turning out as I vaguely surmised they might, but I soon realized that it would be best for Edwin Drood to keep out of sight. She was still deeply in mourning for her brother at that time and could well have held me in some way responsible for his death had I declared myself — and it soon became obvious, in any case, that the possibility of *any* nephew of John Jasper making headway with that particular lady stood very little chance of success! Apart from anything else, I soon realized that Mr Crisparkle, a man whom I've always admired, was paying court to her and it seemed best, in the circumstances, that I should complete my commission as soon as I could and steal quietly away into the night. I gather, in fact, that Mr Grewgious presented the picture to them both as a wedding present.'

'And while on the subject of weddings,' said Holmes, 'are you able to enlighten us as to what became of a certain engagement ring?'

'I returned it to Mr Grewgious, when I stumbled into his office on the morrow of that attack. He kept it in his safe thereafter, for to have revealed its existence would have been tantamount to acknowledging, of course, that he knew what had become of me. In his last days, rather than raise any old skeletons so far as Rosa was concerned, he passed it to Bazzard to do with as he thought best.'

'And its present whereabouts?' enquired Holmes.

'I thought, Mr Holmes,' exclaimed a beaming, blushing, giggling Rosa Tartar, 'that nothing escaped your eagle eye. Why it's *here*, of course! — where it ought to have been years ago, if only Eddy and I had not been so silly!' And, delighted as a schoolgirl, she held out her left hand for our inspection.

17

Later that night, in a private sitting-room at the Strand Hotel, Holmes introduced the Dean and his wife to the plump little woman who had once been Rosa Bud and then, much to their astonishment, to the bearded French artist who had once been Edwin Drood. There was much embracing and weeping between the two ex-pupils of the Nuns' House seminary and an awkward shaking of hands on the part of the two men, for Mr Crisparkle gazed at M. Dupont in a wonderment not untinged with a certain degree of anger. The artist was speedily prevailed upon to tell his story once again, however, indicating why (in his opinion, and also in that of Mr Grewgious) it was considered impossible for Edwin Drood to proclaim himself alive on his return to England in 1871, and the Dean and his wife listened to him with a steadily increasing sympathy and understanding (although Helena pursed her lips, and had a most curious expression on her face, when he recalled the occasion on which he had painted her portrait).

'So the long and the short of it', said the Dean at last, 'is that *nobody* killed Edwin Drood — except, in a sense, M. Dupont — and for establishing that basic fact, Mr Holmes, we shall be everlastingly grateful to you. But are you now in a position to tell us who was responsible for that murderous attack?'

'In one sense,' said Holmes, 'there is no great secret about the matter. It was indeed, as Mr Datchery had surmised, John Jasper who endeavoured to remove Edwin Drood from the face of this earth, in the most literal of fashions.' He paused for a moment and gazed unseeingly at the room's smouldering fire. 'But if we ask ourselves', he continued, *'why* he carried out that terrible assault we are confronted with a strangely complex situation. It is one which I am, indeed, scarcely competent to penetrate. The mind of that man could be likened, perhaps, to a dark cavern in which dreams jostle with reality for supremacy, but it might be more rewarding if we were to think of it, in the first instance, as two separate caverns which share a common entrance and, let us say, a short length of corridor but which thereafter completely diverge. Two totally distinct identities, as it were, inhabit the same body and bear the same name but are unaware of each other's existence.

'Problems of nomenclature, to digress for a moment, have been a curious feature of this investigation. Mr Drood was christened Edwin but was known to his uncle as Ned and to his fiancée as Eddy and he has now acquired — and proposes to retain for evermore, I assume — the name of Edmund. When a poor old woman visited Cloisterham twenty-six years ago she came with the express purpose of warning someone called Ned that his life was in danger, but being unable to track down such a person she passed the time of day with a young man called Edwin, who thoughtfully gave her three shillings and sixpence.'

'I remember her!' exclaimed Drood-Dupont, in great excitement. 'She did indeed manage to warn me, after a fashion, for she told me that Ned was a dangerous name to bear and that it was a threatened name. I remember her very well — she reminded me, in some peculiar fashion, of Jack, for she had a curious seizure while we spoke and it was similar to one which Jack himself had experienced in my presence.'

'The reason being,' said Holmes, 'that both of them were addicted to the drug of opium and it was, indeed, their common craving that brought them together. The Princess Puffa, as she was known in less salubrious circles, was able to keep your uncle — the darker side of him, that is — supplied with the stuff, and he frequently patronized the den over which she presided. You referred to him just now, M. Dupont, as Jack although the rest of us have tended to think of him as John — but Jack is a common enough alternative, as Watson here will readily testify! You yourself, M. Dupont, have lived a double life in the sense of two separate existences, but one of them followed close upon the heels of the other whereas your uncle lived two separate existences simultaneously.

'It may simplify matters,' he continued, 'if we refer to the two personalities as Good Mr Jasper and Bad Mr Jasper. Good Mr Jasper was the gentleman who served as music-master in the town of Cloisterham and choir-master in its Cathedral, who was intelligent and courteous, respected by his associates and revered by his housekeeper. He was renowned, moreover, first and foremost, for being extremely fond of his nephew. Bad Mr Jasper, on the other hand, was the violent character who visited opium dens and (I suspect) other places of ill repute and was the man who terrified Miss Rosa Bud and aroused the contempt of Miss Helena Landless. The passion that dominated Bad Mr Jasper, above all others, was a terrifying hatred and resentment of his nephew. The reasons for this can only be surmised. Edwin, let us say, had been unwittingly responsible for the death of Bad Mr Jasper's sister and had afterwards supplanted him in the affections of Bad Mr Jasper's parents. Finally, and most crucial factor of all, Edwin was betrothed to Miss Rosa Bud, a young lady for whom Bad Mr Jasper had developed an intense desire. These are, as I conceive it, the basic factors that motivated Bad Mr Jasper into carrying out the murder of his nephew. It was Bad Mr Jasper, too, who somehow contrived to make a copy of the key to the Sapsea tomb, concealing it in a place where the Good Mr Jasper would never find it. It was Good Mr Jasper, on the other hand, who devoted himself to the task of bringing the Murderer to justice.'

There was silence for some moments. 'I seem to recall', said M. Dupont at last, in shaken tones, 'Mr Grewgious depicting for me, on one occasion, what he took to be the character of a true lover. He described him, if I remember aright, as "living at once a doubled life and a half life" — a description that seems terribly apt so far as poor Jack is concerned!'

Holmes nodded. 'The transition from one personality to

the other', he said, 'appears to have been strangely abrupt, and where one ceased and the other commenced, and the frequency at which such transitions occurred, are matters which are, I fancy, almost impossible to determine.

'But it would seem that, within a year of the apparent murder of Edwin Drood, the wall that separated the two Mr Jaspers was wearing strangely thin and that possession of their common outer shell (almost equivalent, indeed, to a tomb in its own right!) was taken first by one and then the other in bewildering rotation. It was Bad Mr Jasper who set out for the churchyard, on the Christmas Eve of 1870, but Good Mr Jasper who was in charge at the point when he left the gatehouse – for he failed to bring with him the key that would open the sepulchre. It was Bad Mr Jasper who went unerringly to the Sapsea tomb, and groped for the missing key, but it was Good Mr Jasper who recognized, as he thought, the figure of his nephew's murderer standing there and hurled himself upon Helena Landless. An appalling cataclysm then occurred and it is probable that the two Mr Jaspers fused together in frightful unity for a time. Later, they once again separated, but the wrecked personality whom the outside world knew as Mr Jasper was left, I surmise, with a faint recollection that someone who (in Bad Mr Jasper's eyes) might have been Edwin, had confronted him in what must have seemed a ghastly dream – that the three of them, as it were, had met together once more, for the last time – and thereafter was seeking reassurance and definite confirmation, one way or the other, of what had become of Edwin.

'But these are', he concluded, 'the conjectures of one who

is an amateur in this particular field, which is more properly, indeed, the province of my friend and colleague here, and I put it to you as a working hypothesis and nothing more.'

Those present, myself included, shook their heads in wonder at this strange assessment and, little by little, some further recollections of episodes involving Mr Jasper, tending to confirm the validity of Holmes's diagnosis, were brought to light. A mystery that had endured for a quarter of a century (and had seemed, indeed, destined to endure indefinitely) had finally been cleared up. Wonderment was replaced, after a time, by heartfelt relief among our four companions and it was clear, as their conversation became more general and happier memories were recalled, that the long separation between the Crisparkles and Rosa was at an end and that there would be, henceforth, a close relationship between the two couples. (Just how close would be demonstrated some eighteen months later, when I drew Holmes's attention to an item in the *Telegraph* announcing the engagement of Miss Florence Tartar to Mr Neville Crisparkle.) Refreshments were supplied by the management of the Strand Hotel and it was, indeed, a singularly convivial gathering that finally came to an end as the witching hour approached. 'And pray give our esteemed regards', said Holmes, as we took our leave, 'to Sir Thomas Sapsea.' There was a roar of laughter at this and as the door closed behind us I could almost swear, save for the sheer impossibility of the thing, that I heard the words 'Old Tory Jackass!' escape the lips of the Dean.

When we returned to Baker Street, soon after midnight, we found a further telegram from Stazeby Nanton awaiting us. It bore the news that John Jasper had been found lying in a field within two miles of the asylum, that he was suffering from acute pneumonia and was not expected to survive for more than twenty-four hours.

18

'There is,' said Holmes, 'one last service you can perform for John Jasper.'

'For that man? Never!' exclaimed the Dean, his normally open countenance darkening.

'For those *two* men,' said Holmes, 'for John Jasper is, as you surely appreciate by this time, a divided personality. It is your duty, Mr Crisparkle, to relieve a soul in torment.'

It was the following morning and we had called once more at the Strand Hotel to inform Mr and Mrs Crisparkle of the life that Jasper had been leading at Stazeby Nanton, including his 'unauthorized departures', and to acquaint them with the latest developments. The Dean swallowed hard but nodded, his momentary intransigence at an end. 'You are quite right, of course,' he said. 'Please continue, Mr Holmes. What do you wish me to do?'

'You are to go without delay to Stazeby Nanton and greet John Jasper as an old friend, as though it were 1870 and you had seen him but recently. Appear unaware of his illness. Tell him afresh that Rosa Bud is about to be married and tell him again the tale of the ring which Edwin Drood had been carrying on his person on the Christmas Eve of 1869. So far as *I* am concerned, that is all you have to do — but it may well be that some additional duties will suggest themselves.'

'A singular request!' exclaimed Mr Crisparkle. 'If the man *is* mortally ill, what is the point of this elaborate pantomime? And if he is *not* ill, he must surely be too weak to escape for a fourth time! Are you expecting a death-bed confession of some kind? I'll go, by all means, but I am not at all clear what useful purpose these tales will serve.'

'Not *tales*, Dean, for Rosa is indeed about to be married, and you can say, if you wish, that she is to wed a middle-aged artist called Edmund Dupont, but humour me in my strange designs. I agree that a death-bed confession is unlikely, although it is something that we would be ill advised to rule out completely, but I wish to try an experiment which may result in an even greater degree of relief — not only for ourselves but also for John Jasper.'

'And you will accompany me?' asked the Dean, compliant but still puzzled.

'No, our business lies elsewhere today — but, most certainly, our thoughts will be with you!'

Like the Dean, I was unable to discern the purpose of this exercise, but I knew better than to seek, at this stage, further information from Holmes. That night we returned to Cloisterham, exactly a year since we had first visited the little town, and commenced our Christmas Eve vigil in the Cathedral churchyard, a short distance from the Sapsea tomb. An hour went by, and then another. The moon rose high, though encompassed with clouds, and the

173

night grew colder. I was finally about to suggest to my companion that we must surely be on a fruitless errand, when the moon broke through and I was aware of his sharp intake of breath.

A figure had appeared. It was that of John Jasper, but of a John Jasper we had never seen before — a young man, smartly attired, adorned with lustrous black hair but with an expression of stern intensity on his countenance. He paused for a moment, produced a large key from beneath his cloak, and then approached the tomb.

'Holmes,' whispered I, 'this is something diabolical!'

But Holmes was not listening. He had stepped out, and now confronted the apparition face to face. 'Edwin Drood is not here,' said Holmes distinctly. 'He has escaped from the grave. He is free of you for ever.'

The apparition's face was convulsed with a terrible expression of rage and there burst from it a frightful cry — or, at least, there surely must have done, had we been granted the ears to hear it. And on that instant it ceased to exist.

And at that moment, so the Dean afterwards informed us, as he kept his parallel vigil at the bedside, there died in the Stazeby Nanton asylum an old man called John Jasper, a look of contentment on his face and at peace, at long last, with the world.

'A fetch,' remarked Holmes, as we took our seats in the train bound for London later that night. 'A ghostly double that appears at the moment of death — a quite well attested

174

phenomenon, although I was doubtful of my ability to raise it.'

He puffed at his pipe, as the train gathered speed, although not so contentedly as I had expected. On my congratulating him on the success of his investigations he shook his head in a restless fashion. 'I do not flatter myself', he said, 'that I have got completely to the bottom of the mysterious double life of John Jasper. I suspect that things happened in Cloisterham, Watson, during the lifetime of that strange man, of which you and I can have no conception. Perhaps, so many years after the event, it is best to let sleeping dogs lie – although in this instance, if we bear in mind the curious tale of Durdles concerning the Christmas Eve of 1868, there *was* a dog that did something in the night-time.' He shook his head yet again. 'A strange business,' he murmured.

'And are you able to shed any light, Holmes, on the identity of Dick Datchery?'

'Oh, that! A commonplace little problem, although its wider implications (if any) are obscure. The stroke across the 't' of the name Datchery had been added, you will recall, as an afterthought – the name that originally appeared in that hat had been Dalchery, an anagram of 'Charley D'. It may be that the gentleman in question thought that he would be rumbled too quickly if he adopted the name Dalchery, but who this gentleman was – and why he should equip himself with the Christian name of Dick and disappear so abruptly (at the midway point of the proceedings, as it were) – is something that I am unable to fathom. But it is not worth, I suspect, any further cogitation on our part.'

I was obliged to confess myself similarly baffled. Holmes knocked out his pipe, dismissed the problem as a matter of no great consequence and, as the train rumbled on its way, composed himself for sleep.